THERE`LL COME A TIME

by

TERRY CUBBINS

ISBN: 1478104880
ISBN 13: 9781478104889

PROLOGUE

April 1974
South China Sea

I was standing the midnight watch alone on the ships` bridge when I first noticed the blip on the radar screen. Taking a closer look, I could see the contact was twenty miles away and moving towards us on a reciprocal heading. That was the nice thing about radar; it keeps ships *passing* in the night, not *crashing* in the night.

The other crew members were below deck, asleep in the tons of marijuana bales we had stuffed in every nook and cranny aboard the 115-foot boat *Intrepid*. We were sailing in an area of the South China Sea that was probably the heaviest as far as pirate activity went but we were hoping we could just whistle our way through until we reached the northern tip of the Philippine Islands; from there we'd catch the currents of the great circle route back to San Francisco. We were armed but I didn't consider any of us dangerous.

Before looking at the radar again, I thought back to the job description I was given before hiring on for this insane adventure: *"If you really wanna help your brother, all you gotta do is take a boat to Malaysia, refuel, swing by Thailand, then head home. It takes about sixty days…you stand some wheel watches…get tan… catch some fish…and we pay you plenty. We do it all the time. Whadda you say?"*

More than once I considered my sanity for taking this job, but there wasn't a lot I could do about my decision now, I was the only engineer aboard and it was up to me to keep the boat running. But with every glance at the radar, I was growing a little more nervous; the blip on the screen was maintaining its heading and closing quickly.

Cal, the captain, had issued orders not to change course unless it was an emergency; he said we needed to keep to a schedule. Well, I knew that if we smashed into that guy out there, it would definitely put a crimp in our schedule. So I tweaked the autopilot a tad and changed course…did a little zig as it were. I waited a while before checking the radar again.

Hmm…the guy has done a little zig himself…Okay, I'll zag back.

I gave it a few minutes then looked at the screen again. *Damn, he's done the same thing!*

I hoped this was one of those instances when you bump into somebody coming out of a door or on a sidewalk. You know, when you both move in the same direction at the same time? "Oops, excuse me! Nooo, excuse *me!*" You do this little dance, laugh, then go on your way.

But I was getting a feeling that wasn't the case, it was like the guy out there in the dark wanted to see us about something. I gave it another five minutes and checked the radar again. *Damn…it's still coming our way.*

I thought about the newspaper article I had read in Malaysia; it was about a local kid who was caught with one pound of pot. He was given a quick trial for possession of marijuana and found guilty. He was executed.

I guess I'd been naive about the drug laws in this part of the world but they're quite clear: if you're guilty of possession of one pound or more of marijuana…you die. *One pound?* No appeals, no nothing. Simple business.

I checked the radar again. Whatever was out there was down to six miles and still closing.

It was time to wake the crew.

CHAPTER ONE

As a kid growing up in Seattle I looked up to my older brother Tim. Unfortunately a lot of the time I was looking up at him from the ground because that's where he'd just knocked me. It seemed we just couldn't get through a day without getting into a fight. I guess I asked for a lot of the thumpings the way I followed Tim around, always pestering him. He was a year and a half older than me, which in that time of our lives put him at a big advantage.

We lived in a modest two-story house in a middle class neighborhood in the area known as West Seattle, and if you looked closely from my bedroom window, you could see between the tops of the neighbor's trees and get a glimpse of Elliot Bay and the city. We were thrilled when we realized we could watch the construction of the Space Needle from that window.

Our dad had died in a boating accident not long after I was born and our mom worked two jobs trying to raise us so there wasn't always a referee around to break things up.

But that all changed the night our mother invited Kenny, an engineer from Boeing to our house for dinner.

Kenny wasn't a bad looking guy, about six foot tall, wavy brown hair with a little Kirk Douglas action on his chin. He even wore a sports jacket over a white shirt the night he came to dinner. Looked downright respectable.

Things had started off well enough with the four of us at the kitchen table. Our mom had served the spaghetti and sat down. Kenny held an open bottle of red wine and was waiting to pour. He had obviously had a couple of drinks before he got to our house, the way his hand was shaking, and when he reached over to pour my mother's wine, he spilled half of it on the tablecloth.

“Shit. Sorry about that,” he said as he clumsily tried to wipe it off.

Our mom blushed and said, “Oh, don’t worry about it. Sit still, I’ll get it.” She jumped up to get a wash cloth.

“Hey! You said shit!” I proclaimed as only an eight year old can.

“Sonny Williams, you watch your mouth,” my mother said sternly, as she returned to the table and began wiping up the spill.

“Bette, here, I’ll do that.” Kenny said as he reached for the cloth, bumping her arm. Mom knocked the bottle of wine over, sloshing into his lap.

“Jesus Christ! Kenny said, jumping up from the table.

I exploded into laughter which sent Tim to giggling as well. But all laughter stopped when Kenny grabbed Tim by the arm.

“You think its funny do you? You think it’s funny you little shit?” He began twisting Tim’s arm.

“Kenny, please don’t…” My mom stepped towards him.

“It’s not so funny now is it!?” Kenny’s face was inches from Tim’s and turning purple.

My mother grabbed Kenny’s arm but he just flung her away with his free hand.

I jumped up and started throwing punches at him.“Don’t you touch her! Let go of my brother!”

Kenny cuffed me on the side of my head, sending me flying back into my chair.

“Stop it! Stop it!” my mother screamed and again pulled Kenny’s arm. When Kenny backhanded her I went ballistic. I grabbed the closest thing to me, which happened to be a plate of spaghetti, and fired it at him as hard as I could. It caught him high on the forehead and knocked him backwards, enough for Tim to break free.

Stunned, Kenny groaned and slumped back against the kitchen counter, spaghetti hanging in his eyes, red sauce dripping down his white shirt. We all backed away from him and I realized that something didn't look right with his head; his wavy hair wasn't where it was supposed to be.

My God! I've sliced open his scalp!

Then when I looked closer it dawned on me. *It was a hairpiece. He was wearing a hairpiece!*

Kenny gasped and tried to speak but it just came out in sprayed spittle and sounded like; "Burble."

With spaghetti still wedged between his scalp and hairpiece, he shuddered a couple of times then flustered his way out the back door.

Our mother immediately grabbed us, crying and apologizing over and over. When the sniffling slowed, we took a breath, looked at each other…and started laughing uncontrollably.

We made a pact right then and there; we will always stick together, there`ll be no more fighting…and no more spaghetti heads.

CHAPTER TWO

As we grew older and entered high school, Tim shot up to a skinny six foot-one, black hair with a widow's peak that according to him, made girls dizzy.

Since the Kenny episode, Tim had taken his role as, `man of the house` seriously and as soon as he got his drivers license he bought a light green, '51 GMC pick-up truck and began delivering newspapers, hauling trash, or whatever else he could hustle up. Every week he'd put something into the house kitty. I knew my mom was very proud of him.

I wasn't as tall as Tim and didn't have the widow's peak, but I had the same black hair and the same mother's love that he did. Plus, I had filled out enough to whip his ass if I wanted to. In fact, I almost felt cheated: after those early years of being the little brother, I had finally caught up to him. I still looked up to my brother, but now it was from eye level and revenge just did not seem right.

When the Viet Nam war ramped up to full tilt, it seemed like everybody around us was being drafted. If you were seventeen or eighteen and trying to plan your future, you had to factor in the war one way or the other.

Tim was 4-F due to kidney problems but I was considered prime beef and right in the middle of the lottery. I knew Tim didn't want me to go to Nam and told me one day, "Listen, Nixon's not going to end this war anytime soon and I'd rather see you heading north to Canada than going over there. I don't want you to get shot-up in a jungle that's half way around the world. And as far as I know, nobody on this side of the ocean cares about that damn place. At least anybody we know." He paused for a moment, "I'll go with you if you want…to Canada that is."

While I appreciated the offer, I told him that since I was going to be drafted anyway, I might as well choose which branch of the military I would serve in.

On a cold, wet November day, Tim drove me downtown to the navy's recruiting office where I would be sworn in and sent on my way. We rode mostly in silence but when we pulled up to the curb, Tim said, "I'll make you a deal, if you take care of yourself, I'll take care of Mom."

"It's a deal." I said. "Just remember…"

"…no spaghetti heads!" we both finished.

As we stood beside the car in the rain, we shook hands, then almost awkwardly, we hugged each other.

CHAPTER THREE

My military orders did take me to the jungles, although they were the jungles near the U.S. Naval station in Subic Bay, Philippines. I was assigned to a small fleet of tugboats where I trained to become an engineer, and while I was grateful I wasn't being shot at, the sweltering humidity and oppressive heat in the tug's engine room had me wondering at times how the people in Canada were doing.

The years of my enlistment went by well enough and I was able to go home on leave a couple of times. Tim had taken a job driving truck for a local delivery service and although he had a girlfriend and his own apartment, he still found time to stop by our mother's house for dinner a couple of nights a week. Everything seemed to be all right at home.

By the time I was discharged, Tim owned two small trucks and had started his own delivery service. He wanted me to go into business with him but since his venture was still new, I thought it best to take the job I had been offered by a tugboat outfit, at least for a while. The company towed barges all around the world and I'd be at sea most of the time, which would be ideal for saving money, money that I could invest in Tim's company if things worked out.

It wasn't a bad plan, and the first year went well.

But then things began to unravel.

We were five miles off the entrance to the Miami harbor, coming from Puerto Rico with a four hundred foot barge in tow. We had just begun the slow-down procedure to let the million ton, brake-less monster directly behind us lose momentum, when the captain called me to the wheelhouse.

"Sonny, we just got a message from Miami dispatch. You need to call home as soon as we hit port."

A knot formed in my stomach.

Three hours later we had the barge secured and tied up to a pier in Biscayne Bay. I found a pay phone at the end of the pier and called Tim. He answered on the second ring.

"Hello."

"Hey, it's me. What's up?"

The silence on the other end of the line had my heart racing.

"Mom's dead."

My breath caught in my throat.

"She…she was killed crossing the street in front of our house. Some bastard just ran her down. Didn't even slow down."

I don't know how long I stood there staring into space, but finally I heard my brother's voice coming from a distance.

"Sonny, Sonny, you there?" I still had the phone in my hand but it was against my chest. "Sonny? Sonny, can you come home?"

CHAPTER FOUR

I looked for Tim in the mass of faces that had deplaned in Seattle at the Sea-Tac airport. Amidst the crowd, I almost walked right by him. He was still as skinny as ever but now his hair was long and he sported a bushy mustache. Our handshakes worked into hugs and we embraced without saying anything. When we finally stepped back from each other there were tears running down both our faces. We didn't know what to say. Finally, Tim just shook his head slowly. There was no way our mother should be dead.

Eventually, we straightened up and agreed that a shot of whiskey was in order.

We stayed at the airport bar longer than we should have. When I asked Tim about his girlfriend, Lori, he said she was okay, then after a pause he added, "I hired her brother to drive for me. I guess you could say it wasn't one of my best moves."

When I asked how business was going he just looked at his drink and didn't say anything. The conversation didn't get any better when I asked him about his kidney problem.

"Aw, it's okay…for now. It's nothing I want to talk about now." He stood up and drained his glass. "We better get outta here while one of us can still drive."

A few days after the funeral, Tim and I were mentally zapped. We'd cried every tear we could. We were sitting at the round oak table in the kitchen, the same table that witnessed the K.O. of

Kenny. The strain of the funeral had taken it's toll, but we were beginning to come out of the fog.

It was early afternoon when Tim opened his second beer of the day. "Well, I can't think of anything else. Can you?" he asked, leaning back in mom's favorite chair. It was a rickety wooden thing that Dad had refurbished when they were first married.

"No…no I think we've done all we can. Obit, bills..." a list scrolled through my mind, "shit, I don't know Tim."

Probably thirty seconds of silence went by before Tim said, "I might as well tell you…"

Suddenly, the knot in my stomach grew again.

"Your kidneys?" I asked.

"Yeah. I might be a candidate for a transplant."

I was stunned. "Well, that's great. But you know, I've got a couple of kidneys myself. Both of 'em work really well. How many you need?"

Tim nodded, smiled and said, "Thanks, bro. I hope it doesn't come to that, but thanks."

"We'll beat this, just like we do everything else," I said. "Fuck `em, no spaghetti heads!" I raised my glass, "And just to make sure my kidneys match up with yours, I'll have another beer!"

We laughed and toasted each other.

A moment passed, then Tim took a deep breath and said something else that stunned me. "You asked me how my business was doing? Well, I can tell you it wasn't worth a shit when I first started."

"But it picked up?"

"Yeah, it picked up considerably…once I started hauling pot."

I almost spit out my beer. "You're shittin` me, right?"

"Brother, I wish I was, I certainly hadn't intended to get mixed up in anything like that. But a while ago, Lori asked me if I could find work for her brother, Jamie. He'd dropped out of college and was having a hard time finding anything. I've known him for a while and liked him. I thought he was a good kid. He's about six-foot, blond hair, kinda looks like a tennis pro, but doesn't act like one. Point is, he looked like he could handle the work. I hired him to make Lori happy. At the time I had a contract haulin` marine equipment down I-5 to Portland. It was only once a week and was an easy run, so I let Jamie start off there.

"At first there wasn't any problem but after a while I noticed that on some trips Jamie was taking longer than usual to make the run down and back. I checked the logs and mileages and they just weren't jivin'. I thought maybe he was getting lost on the way and didn't want to tell me. But damn, who can't make it to Portland? Then after he came back from one of his trips, I found coffee grounds in the back of his truck. That made me squirm a little. Something was up. I made up my mind to ask him about it but the next day I had to go to the clinic for tests and I kinda forgot about it.

"Look, I was shook up when the doctor told me how serious things could get. I was even more shaken when I found out how much a transplant operation would cost. I checked with my insurance company but they decided this was all a `pre-existing condition` or something like that. Tough shit in other words. I dropped the bastards.

"I couldn't pay my bills let alone a ga-jillion dollar operation. I thought about selling my trucks but I knew I wouldn't get much for them. I didn't say anything to Mom or anybody but Lori knew something was up. Finally I told her. She was worried, but neither of us had an answer, so we decided to keep working. I could only hope the meds worked and that the next lab test would be okay.

"Not long after that, Jamie came to me and asked if there was anything he could do. Obviously Lori had told him what was goin` on, but I just kinda shook him off and said no, not unless he had fifty thousand or so in his pocket.

"Well, his reaction got my attention. He just stood there and nodded, almost like he was considering it. That's when I knew something was going on, so I told Jamie that I knew what he'd been doing with my truck. I was bluffing of course and hoping for an argument, you know, a-what the-hell-are-you-talking-about kinda thing. But when his shoulders sagged and he shook his head, I knew I had hit on something. I was disappointed. I liked the kid, still do. I was hoping I was wrong."

I sat there mesmerized by what Tim was telling me and where this was all leading. Tim paused for a moment, took a swig of beer, and then continued with his story.

"Well, Jamie broke down and told me the whole story. He *was* driving pot. A friend of his from college knew he was making runs to Oregon and asked Jamie to drop off a package for him. Jamie would get five hundred dollars for his troubles. Of course it was supposed to be a one-time thing, but you can guess how that works.

"At first he was dropping the pot off to a guy near Portland, but when the loads starting getting into the two hundred pound range, Jamie started driving them up the Columbia River to a farmhouse outside the town of Mount Hood. The same guy would help him unload, give him any cash from the previous loads, then Jamie would hightail it back, trying to make up time.

"I was pissed. Finally Jamie asked me what I was gonna do. Was I was gonna tell Lori? Was I was gonna turn him in or something?

"I told him to get the hell out of my sight, I'd see him in the morning. But before he got to the front door I asked Jamie how much he made at my expense. I was floored when he said almost twenty-five thousand!

"The next morning Jamie showed up and handed me nearly seventeen thousand dollars. Told me it was all mine, no questions, no hard feelings. Told me how sorry he was about everything. Then he asked me if he still had a job."

Tim stopped and looked down at his beer. "I suppose you can guess where all this is going. By the end of the day, Jamie still had a job alright. He also had me as a partner. I figured I'd let him roll until I could pay off the bills and put a down payment on a kidney."

I couldn't help it, I laughed. "Tim, you can't even put a down payment on a camper."

"Very funny," Tim said with a smile. "Well everything went smooth for a while, then *bam*, it got scary. Jamie had just off-loaded at the farmhouse and was driving down the dirt road that leads back to the highway. The guy at the farmhouse had given him an unusually large amount of cash to take back and Jamie was a little uneasy. He had every reason to be. Just as he got to the highway, a car that was coming down the blacktop suddenly swerved over and pulled up right in front of him, blocking the road. Two guys in Nixon mask's jump out, guns drawn."

Tim saw my reaction. "I swear to God Sonny, I'm not making this up. They grabbed Jamie outta the cab and slammed him face down on the ground. It was over in about thirty seconds and they drove off. It scared the shit outta Jamie."

My head was spinning. "This is serious shit, Tim. What have you got yourself into?! Or better yet, what are you doin` to get out of it?"

"Well, the guy Jamie is working for, feels that Jamie's somewhat responsible for losing the cash. And that's *after* Jamie gives `em back all the cash we had!! They think Jamie could have driven around the bad guys or backed up or something, I dunno. It was ninety-five thousand, by the way."

"Wait a minute. Bad guys? To have *bad* guys, you have to have *good* guys. I'm a little confused here!"

"Yeah, I know, but there's..."

"Besides, whadda you care? You and Jamie are done right? You walk away, your career in crime is over. Lesson learned."

"If only. The guy Jamie answers to, they call him the old man, says if Jamie is still interested in making some money, and show he didn't have anything to do with what went down, he'll make one more trip for him."

"Yeah. sure, and then it's a done thing right?...Bullshit."

"One trip, two hundred thousand."

The amount was staggering.

"Two hundred thousand to make *one* trip in a truck? Where do you have to drive to, Hawaii?"

Tim laughed, "You're close, but it's not in a truck, it's in a boat. And it's heading to Thailand."

"Haven't you heard about Thai prisons? Jesus, Tim, they kill people for this shit. There are no fair trials. No hot-shot lawyers. You rot man. Jamie's not gonna do it is he?"

"No. He said they wanted him to make the trip because he knew diesel engines, but no, he can't even cross Puget Sound on a ferry without getting seasick."

"Good for him. Sounds like the kid's got some smarts after all."

Tim hesitated, "Yeah, well…he's not going…I am.

CHAPTER FIVE

It's funny how life works. One minute you've got everything laid out in front of you and you have a general idea which direction you're headed. You think you've got a handle on things. Then a huge detour sign pops up right in front of you.

It makes you wonder who's really in charge here.

For over an hour I listened to Tim tell me why he was even considering risking life and limb, to say nothing of a huge jail sentence, to undertake such an venture.

"It only takes a month to sail over, a month to sail back." Tim said, obviously reciting what Jamie had told him.

"They put the boat on autopilot and cruise across the ocean. You catch a lot of fish and get a nice tan; doesn't sound too hard to me. `Course, there's a little more to it than that."

"You think?" I asked.

"I know there`d be some risks."

"*Some* risks?"

"Yeah, well, they say we might be going through an area known for pirates. And then when you actually load and off-load, those times are crucial too I guess, but apparently these guys have got their shit together and do it all the time. Jamie said, that according to the old man, all the loading and off-loading is done on the high seas, so it's probably not even illegal."

"Not illegal?! Of course it's illegal! I can't believe you're even considering any of this. Besides, you don't know anything about boats!"

"Sure I do... `member that summer I fished in Alaska?"

"You were the *cook* for Christ's sake!"

"Yeah, well how hard can it be? And another thing, Jamie said if anything should happen, which it never has by the way, he said they'd make it good, meaning I'd get paid no matter what. Plus they'd take care of any legal expenses…long as I keep my mouth shut of course."

"You mean like if you get caught and sent to jail for ten years, they'll pay for the lawyer? Wow, how can you resist that?"

"Look Sonny, I got myself into this mess, I'll get myself out of it."

"Aren't you forgetting something? What about the little matter of your health? What if you get sick while you're in the middle of the ocean? There are no magical kidney boats that will show up and save the day."

"Actually I thought about that. I'm thinking some clean ocean air, exercise, and a healthy diet of fresh fish might do me a world of good. Who knows, maybe I'll put on some weight, maybe this is just what I need?"

"Sure, we'll just look at this as a very risky way to get healthier. The newest diet craze; running from drug lords. I can't believe you're seriously considering doing this. When is this supposed to happen?"

"The boat leaves San Francisco in three weeks."

I shook my head.

Three weeks.

That didn't give me much time to talk some sense into him.

CHAPTER SIX

The next few days I spent making phone calls. The first call was to my boss at the tugboat company to ask for a six month leave of absence. I told them I needed the time to straighten out my mother's affairs. I also called the bank and a few realtors. I learned that we owed almost as much on Mom's house as it was worth. A few more calls to health assistance programs and insurance companies were just as discouraging. I even tried contacting a military adviser to see if any of my benefits could extend to my brother. No go.

At the end of one week I had exhausted every option I could think of that might persuade Tim to change his mind. There just didn't seem to be any way to offset the money that was dangling in front of him.

On Friday night, we sat in the kitchen, each of us lost in our own thoughts.

Tim broke the silence. "I'm going. Besides, it's too late now. They have to have a fourth crew member, and I'm it. It might get ugly if I don't go."

"Whoa, whadda you mean, *ugly*? Did they threaten you?"

"No, not exactly..."

"Alright, how about if I go? Would they let me take your place? I can offer a lot more than you when it comes to boats."

"Don't even go there little brother, this isn't your deal."

But go there we did. For the next hour. And it damn near escalated in to a full blown fist fight. Fortunately we both pulled back at the last minute, remembering where we were, remembering our mother. Remembering the pact we made in this kitchen, right here at this table. We agreed to talk about it in the morning.

As Tim started for the back door he suddenly stopped, mussed his hair, and started drooling. Then with great exaggeration, he lurched and staggered his way to the back door.

"Fuck you, `spaghetti head," I said as he let himself out.

It took three more days of talking with Tim but I finally made a deal with him; if he would at least get Jamie to tell the old man about me, then I would quit bugging him. I would accept whatever was said. If they wouldn't consider me to take Tim's place, I'd give up and go away. At least that's what I told Tim.

The next day we had our answer, and I think it surprised both of us; whoever was running this little operation was interested in my engineering skills. If I could be in San Francisco in two days, someone would meet with me, do a little interview. Jamie gave us the name of a motel and said a man named Rex would contact me there. Tim didn't like it at all, and we almost went at it again, but I finally I picked up the Yellow Pages, and booked the flight.

CHAPTER SEVEN

San Francisco

It was a pleasant spring afternoon with just a light breeze blowing when a taxi dropped me off at a motel just outside the city by the bay. It wasn't much of a motel, maybe forty rooms on one level, painted white with blue doors. All very low key except for a sign in the office window which proclaimed, "New, HBO!"

It was getting dark outside when the call came. Rex told me to be outside my door in thirty minutes; he'd pick me up.

I don't know what kind of car I was expecting but I was surprised when a big black Lincoln drove up and stopped in front of my room. A thin, red-haired guy about thirty years old rolled his window down and leaned his head out, a wispy goatee sprouted from his chin."Sonny?"

"Yeah."

"I'm Rex, come on, get in. We're going down to the waterfront."

I jumped in and he gunned the big car towards the city and harbor. *So much for low key.*

On the ride through town Rex explained that for the sake of saving time, our meeting would be on the boat that was going to be used in the operation.

We made our way through the city and down along the Embarcadero. The lights of the city sparkled across the water.

Then with tires squealing we drove into a huge empty warehouse adjacent to a long wharf. Rex stopped the car and turned off the lights. At that point I half expected a couple of goons to appear out of the darkness and say something like, "The boss thinks you know too much. Please step into this wet concrete." But my tensions eased a little after we got out of the car and walked through open roll-up metal doors out onto the wharf.

"Well, there she is. Whadda you think?" Rex said as he nodded towards a lone boat that was riding a low tide, rocking gently against dock pilings.

I was surprised and a little disappointed. The *Intrepid* was an odd looking, maybe thirty year-old boat that had seen better days. The wheelhouse and main cabin sat forward in a normal fashion for a boat her size, but the aft deck and beam seemed narrow in relation with the rest of the boat, giving her a top-heavy, or tender look. I guessed her length to be about 120 feet. She looked like a shipyard had started to build a tugboat with the standard rubber bow pud on her nose and the obligatory tires chained along the rails, but then, halfway through the job, decided she should be an offshore oil rigboat and stretched her aft deck to handle long sections of drill pipe.

Exhaust stacks sat amidships framing the boat with the port stack serving as an entry to the engine room below. She had all the dings and dents of a work boat, listed slightly to starboard, and was...*ugly.*

But what the hell, maybe ugly *is better than slick in this situation. As long as she can take a punch, who cares what she looks like?*

Rex led the way toward the boat. We made our way down a ladder to the aft-deck and then went forward through an open hatch into a narrow crews` lounge. I could see two men seated, beers in hand.

The first guy Rex introduced me to was Cal. Cal was wearing shorts, stood about six-one, and had blond curly hair. He had the shoulders of a linebacker and didn't look to be much more than thirty years old. I was surprised when Rex said he was the captain of the *Intrepid*. He looked more like a captain of a rugby team than a captain of a boat.

The other man's name was Bob. He was about the same age as Cal, but dark complexioned with a Canadian accent. He was built like a middleweight fighter and looked like he could grow a beard in an afternoon. But he had a quick smile and an easy manner about him. Although Rex didn't say what Bob's position was, I figured him for the first mate or deckhand.

I accepted the beer they offered and we all made small talk about San Francisco nightlife and what a great city it was. When we finally we got down to the nitty-gritty I was in for another surprise. I had already been hired.

"The old man says you'll do," Cal spoke up. "He likes your resume. He likes the fact you can handle a wrench as well as a throttle. We'll give you a tour of the boat, make sure it's something you want to do. And just so you know, there`ll be four of us and we all stand wheel watches. But, don't worry about cooking; that's Rex`s job"

I was still shocked at how fast everything was happening. I was basically a man off the street and as far as I knew, these guys didn't know me from Adam. Yet I was being taken in their confidence.

Something didn't seem right.

The next couple of hours were question and answer time with me asking all the questions and the crew of the *Intrepid* all too eager with answers.

"Fuel capacity and range?" I asked.

"Forty thousand gallons and a ten thousand mile range."

"Fresh water supply?"

"Plenty, over six thousand gallons."

"Time since last engine overhaul?"

"Recent on both engines."

"Spare parts?"

"Lot's of `em."

"Generator systems?"

"'A'- okay."

And so it went until I ran out of questions and they ran out of beer. If I had any doubt about the seriousness of the operation, it evaporated when Cal said, "One more thing, we'll have weapons aboard. A couple of AR-15's, a 45 pistol and a 12 gauge shotgun. Not a great arsenal, but it gives us something in case we run into pirates. You okay with that?"

It was something I hadn't thought about, and when I just shrugged, he said, "Good, welcome aboard. We sail in ten days."

On the flight home I went over all the concerns I had about the boat. It sure didn't fit the image I had of something smugglers might use. It certainly wasn't built for speed and lacked any real James Bond high tech stuff. She was powered by twin 1271 Detroit diesels, which if throttled up, might push the her along at a top speed of 12 knots. Certainly not enough to outrun anybody.

And I wasn't crazy about the weapons part of the deal, but I had to admit, I'd rather have them than not if we did encounter pirates.

As I thought about every issue or problem I could imagine, Tim's situation always seemed to trump them. The whole thing was scary, stupid, and against every instinct I had. But Tim was my brother. And family apparently trumped good sense.

Tim picked me up at the airport but waited until we were in his truck and headed home before he asked; "Okay, so whadda' you think? What's it look like?"

I hesitated a second, watching the traffic crawling along with us, then looked at him and shrugged. "Well, unless one of us finds a pot of gold soon, it looks like I'm going on a sea cruise."

CHAPTER EIGHT

The Intrepid

One of my concerns about the whole deal was how I was going to get along for two months at sea with three guys that were not only smugglers but basically strangers as well. It was one thing to work on a tugboat in the navy, but at least I was able to go ashore every few days. Here, aboard the *Intrepid*, that obviously wasn't going to be the case.

I had flown down from Seattle the night before we were to leave port hoping to acclimate myself a little more with the engine room and deck equipment, but Cal insisted on taking the crew to dinner at Fisherman's Wharf. "Screw it", Cal had said when I told him what I wanted to do. "You'll be fine. All you gotta do is start the engines tomorrow morning. There'll be plenty of time to figure things out later. Besides, after tonight, we won't be seeing any women for a while a*nd* we'll have to put up with Rex's cookin' all the way across."

Rex who was standing nearby jumped in. "Well, shit, Cal, I told you if you'd let me bring that waitress I met the other night, she could do the cooking."

"Yeah, but then we'd have to kill her."

At least the two men laughed.

That night at dinner I started feeling a little more comfortable. Maybe it was the food and drinks, but it did seem that Bob, Cal and Rex got along well together. The only thing they argued about was whether Willie Mays should retire or not.

I found out later that Cal and Rex had made the trip before, and although Bob hadn't, I assumed everybody was qualified for the job. Nothing was said about why we were about to take a boat across the Pacific but there were several toasts for a successful voyage. It was almost like we were about to take a vacation cruise.

The next morning at eight o'clock, we were all gathered on the bridge for some last minute instructions from Cal. He seemed a little nervous and fidgety but I thought it was just because of the moment. I was nervous myself and realized that once we cast off, there was no turning back. I didn't know if Cal was reading my mind or not but he surprised me when he said, "Okay guys, anybody wants off, better do it now." It seemed absurd that anybody would change their mind at that point, but for a moment nobody said anything. Then Rex broke the silence, "Let's get goin' Cal, there's some exotic women waiting for me across the pond." Bob laughed and said, "Yeah, and there's some big fish in that pond that I want to catch along the way."

When everybody looked at me, I shrugged and said, "I'll go start the engines."

Ten minutes later I was back on the bridge with Cal. We didn't have an intercom and I knew Cal was waiting for me to report back that everything was up and ready to go. Bob and Rex were standing by on deck to cast off.

"Okay, everything's ready in the engine room," I told Cal. "You want me to help Bob and Rex cast off?"

"Nah, that's okay." Cal said as he nodded toward the pier. "There's a guy on the dock that'll throw off the lines." That's when I noticed a man standing by one of the cleats on the dock. He looked to be about fifty years old, stocky build, and was wearing a San Francisco Giants baseball cap. At first I thought he might have just been passing by, but five minutes later I changed my mind.

With our bow towards shore, Cal gave the order to cast off. As soon as the lines were tossed aboard, Cal reversed one of the engines and brought the stern out away from the pier, but when he tried to bring the bow around, the stern nudged back to the dock. Cal tried another maneuver, but only succeeded in bringing the bow back to it's original position at the pier.

"Goddammit." Cal snapped.

I thought maybe he had forgotten something, and was purposely returning to the dock, but when he tried the same maneuver with the same results, I realized what was happening; a slight breeze and an incoming tide was keeping us pinned to the dock. We had seven thousand miles of ocean to cross but Cal couldn't get us away from the pier! It wasn't until the man on the dock yelled instructions across to Cal that we were finally able to separate ourselves from the pier. After a couple of violent throttle maneuvers that had everyone grabbing something to keep from falling, Cal got the pointed end of the *Intrepid* headed towards the Golden Gate Bridge and the vast Pacific beyond.

I didn't like the way things had started off.

After a couple of days at sea I began to find out that the boat, like Cal, wasn't all it was supposed to be either. On closer inspection of the spare engine parts, I found most of them were worn out, corroded, and in some cases, flat-out broken and of no use at all. The starboard generator ran rough at times and would sometimes go off line, usually in the middle of the night. The port shaft bearing was running hot and the fresh water expansion tank for the starboard engine was leaking.

But the thing that concerned me most was when the fuel oil separator, a centrifuge device that cleaned fuel, gave up seven days out. Without it, I'd be changing filters daily, which in itself was no big deal, but we simply didn't have enough filters aboard the ship to make it across the Pacific.

It seemed the only solution was to make an unscheduled stop in Hawaii and make a time- consuming overhaul on the separator, or pick up a shitload of filters and be on our way. When I told Cal of the situation he was reluctant to the idea of stopping in Hawaii, but I convinced him it was the only answer short of returning to San Francisco.

On the morning of our tenth day at sea we sighted the Big Island. It felt good seeing land again.

I was in the wheelhouse standing behind Cal when we entered the harbor and began our way through the channel to a pier in the distance. We were heading straight for a red channel marker when Cal caught me off guard by asking, "You know which side we're supposed to pass this buoy on?" I wasn't sure if he was kidding or not, but anyone with a grain of salt in their veins has heard the expression, "Red Right Returning." It means you keep the red buoys on your right when returning to port. It helps prevent you from doing embarrassing things...like running aground for instance.

I was a little uncomfortable telling a captain how to run his ship, but when it looked like Cal was going to pass the buoy on our left, I thought I'd better say something. "Ah...skip, I think we better keep the buoy on our right, you know, just to keep enough water under us."

"Oh yeah, right. How deep to you think the channel is?"

"What's the chart say." I asked.

Cal took a quick peek at a chart that was lying on the console. "Hmm, I don't know. I'm not sure."

"How about the depth finder, what's it showing?"

"Ahh...I dunno if it's working right or not."

"Okay, let's just stay to the right of the red buoys and we should have plenty of water."

"You sure? Have you been here before?"

"No, but look up channel. That's about a four-hundred foot freighter that's alongside the pier. If he can make it in here, we should be able to."

"Oh yeah," Cal said, smiling. "Cool!"

Yeah cool, I thought. *And maybe I should just head straight to the airport when we tie up. That is, if we make it to the dock.*

It took Cal a couple of passes at the dock in Hilo, but we were finally able to tie up and go ashore. I found the filters we needed from a nearby marine supply while Rex found a market and restocked the galley with fresh fruit. Bob talked to some locals and bought some fishing lures. Cal stayed on board and tried to figure out what the squiggly lines on the charts meant.

CHAPTER NINE

We all went into town for dinner during our one night layover in Hilo, but this time I felt, more than noticed, a camaraderie with the crew. I still had some serious doubts about a number of things, but I went along with the spirit of the evening. We toasted ourselves several times and patted ourselves on the back for the fine job we'd all done so far. I even decided after a few drinks that Cal wasn't such a bad guy and that he *did* have some navigational skills. *He did find Hawaii, didn't he?* Besides, hopefully from Hawaii to the Philippines there would be no buoys, tides, or parallel parking to worry about. We would be on autopilot crossing a wide open ocean for the next three weeks.

We left the Big Island the next morning, all with the appropriate hangovers, but we left without incident. Maybe it was because there was a slack tide and hardly any wind, but Cal actually handled the boat pretty well this time and he had no problem getting us to open water.

Once we cleared the Islands, we quickly settled back into our routine. We all stood a three hour wheel watch twice a day along with our other duties. Cal kept us on course, Rex kept us fed, Bob supplied us with fresh fish, and I nursed the noises in the engine room.

I don't know if I had a preconceived notion of what drug smugglers were supposed to look or act like, but by the time we were halfway across the Pacific, I felt like the guys I was sailing with were all decent souls. I was pretty sure that they would hold a door open for an old lady.

As the days grew into weeks our pace across the ocean seemed excruciatingly slow. Probably because it was. We were averaging just nine knots which wasn't fast enough to keep boredom away. Day after day the sun blistered the steel decks of the *Intrepid* and when the air-conditioner went tits-up, sleeping below deck meant sleeping in sweat. The sea became so flat that it was dificult to tell where the ocean ended and the sky began. The exhaust from the diesels hung with us, and the closest we came to rain was an occasional thunderhead and a flash of heat lightning off in the distance. We never saw another ship or hint of land. The only people we saw were each other.

But finally, in the early afternoon of our forty-first day at sea, off our port bow, we spotted a mountain peak of one of the Philippine Islands piercing the horizon. The first leg of this journey was almost complete. We had made it across the Pacific.

We stood along the railing in front of the wheelhouse looking into an afternoon sun, mesmerized by tiny summits of mountains inching up out of the ocean. The peaks gradually sloped into dark green, broad shouldered mountains. A while later we could make out waves breaking on a shoreline. Then out of nowhere, hundreds of dolphins appeared, leaping out of the water, racing towards us as if to welcome us to their side of the world.

With dolphins dancing and land growing on the horizon, I had a small tingle of relief knowing that I was almost halfway through this little adventure. If everything went like it was supposed to, Tim would soon have the money he needed, and my career in smuggling pot would be over.

An hour after spotting land we changed course and headed for a passage between islands. Changing course was a cause for celebration in itself. Nobody had touched the automatic pilot in weeks. Our compass had been pointed at 210 degrees for so long we thought maybe it was broken.

We were finally turning.

CHAPTER TEN

Later that night we entered into the chain of islands near the island of Leyte and slipped into the Mindanao Strait. It was pitch black when we made our way through the narrow channel, navigating solely by radar. We couldn't see any buoys but we did notice the radar would intermittently pick up some sort of "glitter" or "clutter", almost like what you might see in heavy weather. Cal dismissed it by saying, "Must be atmospheric conditions."

As we cruised along, we'd see fires along the shore, but other then that there were no sign of life. We settled in and punched the autopilot to take us south towards the Sulu Sea.

Still excited about seeing land and being so close to it we were all gathered in the wheelhouse before dawn the next day, drinking coffee. As daylight slowly filtered through the darkness we began to see what we thought were logs or deadheads floating on the water all around us.

Rex was on watch and just about jumped out of his skin when he put the glasses on one of the logs dead ahead of us. "Holy shit! There's somebody on that log! There's a goddamn face staring back at me!"

He immediately throttled back and eased the wheel to port. Then Bob yelled, "There's another one, starboard side!" Then we began to see them everywhere. In front of us; in back of us; all around us. Slowly we made our way through the flotilla until we realized what was happening, we were steaming right through hundreds of fishermen in tiny dugout canoes.

As the figures slowly materialized we could see men standing in their small boats with nets over their shoulders, bare skin glistening, and …glaring at us.

None of them waved or smiled.

Finally, after we slithered through them and could see our way clear enough to punch in the autopilot again, we all looked back at our wake with the same thought: *Did we swamp any of them in the night?*

Two days later, in the South China Sea, we finally sighted our first port of call, an East Malaysian island called Labuan. The island had just been a dot on the charts we'd all been staring at for over a month, but now as we cruised towards it, the dot took on a personality. We could see palm trees lining white sandy beaches. A green jungle canopy covered small rolling hills and knolls. Wisps of smoke floated up from scattered locations, looking like smoke signals.

It was early afternoon and the weather was as it had been seemingly forever; hot and humid. All four of us were worn out from the first leg of our journey but we were also excited. A cold beer and food cooked by someone else awaited us.

In contrast with the size of the smallish island, we were surprised to see scores of huge oil tankers anchored on the outer reach of the port. Closer towards the island, smaller boats and ships of every description were anchored helter-skelter throughout the horseshoe-shaped harbor.

From about a mile out we could see what looked like a small shipyard on the left side of the bay. To the right, directly across the crowded water, we saw what we had come so far to find; a lone, long wharf jutting out from the belly of a small town.

After a month on a barren ocean, maneuvering through traffic was going to be a bit of a challenge.

Just as we slipped between two anchored scows, a fishing boat, about forty feet long, appeared off our port bow, heading into our path on a ninety degree angle. We could see a deckhand coiling line on the aft deck and another figure in the wheelhouse.

Light blue smoke rose from a dented, gray exhaust stack and the bare woodwork around the cabin looked weathered and rotted.

None of us on the bridge of the *Intrepid* were too concerned as the fishing boat was still a distance away. He wasn't actually fishing, we had the nautical right-of-way, *and* we had the all-important common sense right-of-way...we were bigger than he was.

But as we continued our course, the smaller boat kept chugging away, seemingly oblivious to us.

"I hope this guy catches fish better than he drives a boat," Cal muttered as he stood at the wheel. Normally it wouldn't have been a big deal, but now we were in tight quarters and were running out of room to maneuver.

As both boats continued on their respective courses, Cal grew a little more agitated. "What's up with this guy? He asleep?" Without waiting for an answer, Cal reached up to the overhead and pulled the cord for the whistle; one short blast followed by a longer one.

The deckhand looked up and waved then went back to what he was doing. A moment later, the figure in the wheelhouse stepped out with a hand held air horn and answered us with the identical blast we had just given him, and then stepped back into the cabin. The fishing boat didn't change course.

"What the hell does that mean? What's he doing?"Cal had already throttled back, and had the engines in neutral, but our momentum hadn't slowed much.

Finally, when it was clear that the fishing boat wasn't going to change course, Cal slammed both engines in reverse. "Goddammit, I didn't come all the way over here for a Mexican standoff."

As the boat passed in front of us, Cal stormed out on deck, raised a fist, and yelled, "You lucky little prick! Next time I'll run over your sorry ass!"

The next thirty minutes were much calmer and we threaded our way through the maze without too much trouble. Finally, we approached the end of the pier where there was an open space between two rust-stained fishing boats. Cal brought the *Intrepid* toward the dock but his approach was too shallow and we scraped along the side of one of the fishing boats. Fortunately, the tires hanging down from the *Intrepid's* bulwarks prevented any real damage to either boat, and after a moment, Cal gave up on any fancy parking job park and just nosed the bow of the *Intrepid* into the dock. Bob and Rex jumped onto the wharf and quickly had the boat tied up.

Moments later, in the engine room, I pulled back the throttles on the diesels and listened as they mercifully shuffled to a stop. The engines had been screaming for so long that the sudden quiet was almost eerie.

I listened to the faint hissing, popping and ticking sounds the engines and machinery made as things began a much needed cooling down process. Soaking it in, I smiled knowing I would soon be able to call home. Tim would want to know I was okay.

CHAPTER ELEVEN

I may have shut down the *noise* when I secured the engines but I had also turned up the *quiet*. I began to notice subtle sounds that I hadn't heard in over a month. Water dripping in the bilge and air leaking from one of the compressors brought me back to real time. We'd made it one way across the ocean, which was an accomplishment in itself, but if we were going to make it back, I was going to have to get a lot of work done before we sailed again.

I knew most of the work could be handled without too much trouble if I could get the right parts, but how soon I could get them or whether they were even available in this part of the world was another thing.

Looking around the engine room further and seeing some of the jury-rigged fixes that I had made while on the run, I started to feel a sense a of satisfaction and pride. It slowly occurred to me that what I had accomplished in keeping things running long enough to cross seven thousand miles of open ocean.

"Pat yourself on the back pal...You're doin` a great job. Just like the navy taught you. You keep this up and we'll soon be bringing a huge amount of drugs into the United States! Atta boy!

Then I heard Bob's voice shift through my fog brain. "Hey, Sonny. Come on up. Cal wants to see us all in the wheelhouse."

I pulled a rag out of my back pocket, wiped my hands and headed up the ladder.

❧

"Okay, here's the deal," Cal began once we were gathered around the small navigation table on the bridge. "My instructions are to go ashore and find the hotel Labuan. It shouldn't be too hard to spot; it's supposed to be the only hotel on the island with more than one floor. In fact I bet it's that one right there," Cal nodded to a building rising above a clutter of corrugated rooftops a quarter mile away.

For a moment I visualized how easy Cal would be to spot too as he walked through a crowd with his blond curly locks sticking up a head taller than the short brown-skinned native people swarming around him.

"Anyway, I'm supposed to go ashore and make a phone call from the hotel. I'm not sure where I'm calling, or even who I'm calling, I think it's a number in Thailand, but that doesn't matter. What matters is the people on the other end will tell me where and when we go from here. I'm assuming we'll head for the southern tip of Viet Nam or maybe up towards Cambodia. I'm guessin` well have about four or five days here to refuel and make repairs. It all depends on when the load will be ready and when they want us to pick it up."

He paused long enough to look at me and ask, "That give you enough time for you to do what you gotta do Williams?"

Cal always called me by my last name, although as far as I knew, nobody on the boat knew his.

"If we can find parts, I guess so." I answered.

"Good. Okay, sit tight for now, when I get back you guys can go in and check out the town, have a beer or two."

While Bob, Rex and I waited for Cal to return, we stayed on the bridge and watched the activity going on around us. The pier was about five hundred yards long with four boats tied up to our side and three on the other. Looking through binoculars, I identified a few of the flags the ships were flying; English, Indonesia, Chinese, and French. The smaller fishing boats flew Malaysian colors. It was a real melting pot…except for one; we were the only one flying the red, white and blue of the Stars and Stripes.

I passed the glasses to Rex and wondered to myself if there were any other ships here for the same reason we were.

"S`pose there's any women in town?" Rex asked, aiming the binoculars toward the cluster of buildings in the distance. "I wouldn't mind getting` my oil changed while we're here."

"I dunno Rex, they might think that fuzz on your face is contagious," Bob said.

Rex gave Bob a sideways look, "Well then, they could all be as pretty as me."

Cal had been off the boat for an hour when he finally returned. The tide had gone out a little and he had to make his way down a few rungs of a steel ladder that was attached to the dock. He didn't seem too happy.

We gathered around him in the wheelhouse and he quickly let us know what was up. He'd made telephone contact with the people on this side of the world but apparently the load wasn't ready. He was to call back in five days. Cal seemed a little put off by the news, but we didn't press him for any details. He said I'd be able to get whatever parts I needed from the shipyard across from town but I'd have to take a water taxi over to it. Long, narrow wooden boats, powered by over-sized outboard engines served as taxis and they seemed to be zipping by in every direction.

I could see that Bob and Rex weren't too concerned with the information so I assumed it wouldn't change our schedule too much. I wanted to get this trip over and done with more than anyone aboard, but I was thankful for some time to make repairs. The next leg of our journey was going to be crucial and I wanted to make sure I was doing all I could to keep the *Intrepid* engines and systems operating well enough and long enough to get us back home. Besides we all needed a little R&R. We'd been to sea for a long time and we needed to recharge our own batteries. It was time for a cold beer. It was time to call home.

CHAPTER TWELVE

For all the marine traffic that sat at it's doorstep, the town wasn't much. Along with the five story hotel that overlooked the harbor there were a few grocery stores, a couple of hardware stores, and a half a dozen bars and open air restaurants. Slow moving dogs and scruffy chickens meandered over cracked concrete sidewalks and streets. There was one whitewashed concrete building near the hotel that looked like it could be a school or hospital, or both. If there were any churches or religious temples around, I didn't see them.

Bob and Rex headed for a corner bar that advertised Heineken. As much as I wanted a tall cool one, I told them I'd catch up. First things first, I needed to find a phone.

Cal had said that the only place in town with a land line capable of an international call was at the main hotel so I made my way over to it. As I rounded a corner to the hotel, I froze when I saw the main entrance across the street; standing next to the large double glass doors were two men in military uniforms. I turned and pretended to be interested in something in a shop window and watched their reflection in the glass. Apparently they were just acting as doormen, greeting people as they came and went. A few moments went by before I decided I was just being paranoid. After all, I was just a sailor in town. I had done nothing wrong…yet.

I crossed the street and made my way up the few steps to the door. My apprehension faded a tad as one of the men nodded and held open one of the doors for me. I wasn't sure if they spoke English or not, but I smiled a thank you and passed by them. I wasn't sure if they returned my smile or not, but I probably wouldn't if I had their job.

Stepping into anything air-conditioned was a treat in itself and in contrast to the rest of the buildings in town, the hotel was actually quite nice. At least the lobby was. It was wide and open and probably thirty feet across. Scattered around the atrium were a few over-stuffed chairs with newspaper racks next to them. The only people I saw were a couple of young guys in hotel uniforms, standing casually on the far side of the lobby talking to each other. They didn't appear to be doing anything constructive, and if they were, they were doing it slowly.

My shoes made kind of a squishy, squeaky sound as I walked across a polished marble floor towards the front desk. Off to one side of the lobby I could see an entrance to a bar and dance floor. Next to that was a restaurant with a menu board advertising the special of the day. At the desk I explained to a smiling young lady that I wanted to make a call to the United States. Thankfully she spoke English and told me how to go about placing the call. She then bowed slightly and pointed to a row of telephone booths just past the entrance to the bar.

After sitting in one of the booths for fifteen minutes, listening to different overseas operators, my brother's voice finally came on the line.

"Hello?" he answered, his voice thick and groggy.

"Hey Tim, it's Sonny."

"Oh my God! Where are you? I haven't slept. I've been going crazy back here."

"We're at the halfway point. It was a long hot trip across but we made it."

"Okay, alright, okay. Good to hear. Goddamn it…I've…I've been really worried sick. I shoulda' never let you do it. I'm sorry I got you mixed up in this."

"Well it's too late to worry about all that now. And so far, so far so good. What about you? How you feeling?"

"Oh, I'm okay. The doc wants to do run some more tests but I've been putting him off. I don't want to run up the bill any more than it is already."

It wasn't what I wanted to hear. "Screw the bill!" I shouted. "Do the tests. I'll be home pretty soon and we'll take care of *all* of this."

"Just get home safe okay?"

We chatted a little longer and then he asked me what time it was on my end of the world. It was fourteen hours ahead of him. It was three in the morning in Seattle.

"What's the future look like?" he asked.

"I dunno, bro, but I'm gonna make sure you're around to see it. It'll be nothin` but blue skies from now on."

The next few days went well enough and I was able to find most of the parts I needed. The one disappointment was the air-conditioner. According to a foreman at the shipyard, I'd be lucky to find parts for it in America, let alone East Malaysia. But with Bob's help, I was able to make the major repairs and after five days in port, I felt like we were seaworthy again. We still needed to refuel and take on fresh groceries but those things could wait until just before we sailed. As far as I was concerned we were ready to go.

CHAPTER THIRTEEN

Our excitement of having crossed an ocean began to wear off as the days added up at the dock. Things seemed to be grinding to a halt. We were getting bored. Listless. The tropical heat was relentless and there wasn't enough of a breeze to even stir the palms that lined the shore. The *Intrepid* didn't move unless another boat passed by, usually just a water taxi, and pushed a small wake against her hull causing her to barely wallow.

On one particular languid day, a couple of British sailors stopped by our boat and invited us to a "jolly," or barbeque, out on one of the oil tankers anchored offshore. Because of a recent oil embargo there were at least fifty of these huge vessels sitting idle at anchor, most of them without a crew aboard. These Brit sailors had been hired by the oil companies to periodically check on the tankers and pump bilges, fire up generators, and whatever else was needed to sustain life in a ship. They would typically stay aboard a ship for a week or so, and then move on to check another ship's pulse. It was like the entire fleet of tankers was in an induced coma.

The Brits said they'd invited half the town and would have a launch heading out in the morning if we'd care to join them. They said we could bring a towel and bathing suit if we wanted. *Towel and a bathing suit? More of the tanning time that I was promised in the drug smuggling brochure?*

The rest of the crew declined but I gladly accepted their offer. I had always wanted to see the engine room of a giant oil tanker.

The next morning, I jumped aboard the British launch. The boat was already loaded with about thirty other native men and women, all smiling and laughing and looking forward to the Sunday shindig. As we shoved off and headed out to the party, it amazed me again how many oil tankers there were at anchor. They were stretched out on the horizon as far as you could see. As it turned out, the tanker the jolly was on was the farthest ship away. It took half an hour just to get out to it but we finally pulled up alongside the steel brute. I would later learn from one of the deckhands that the behemoth was almost a thousand feet long, squatted a hundred forty feet wide and could carry enough crude oil to meet the energy needs of the island of Labuan for two years.

Bending my neck and gazing up at this giant reminded me of photographs of the Half Dome in Yosemite. I could see a boarding ladder angling down from the top railing. It hugged the hull for about forty feet to a small platform. From the platform, a rope ladder hung another fifteen feet to the water.

I was the first to start up the ladder. I felt like Spiderman scaling a skyscraper. Soon after beginning the climb, my heart began pounding, my hands started sweating, and a voice inside my head said, "Don't look down."

But jolly it was when I reached the top of the ship's railing and stepped aboard. A very drunk sailor in a wrinkled white uniform warmly greeted me. He wobbled a bit as he turned and pointed me in the direction of the "action" at the base of the ship's bridge. I made my way through a maze of on-deck piping and pumps, and as I got closer I could hear the sounds of music, laughter, and...*splashing?*

After walking the length of several football fields, I finally came to the foot of the bridge. I was shocked by what I saw. There was a mass of people of all shapes, sizes, ages, and colors gathered in and around a modest sized swimming pool! Smoke rose from a couple of barbecues that were being tended by sailors with spatulas in one hand and beers in the other. They were singing loudly off key to the Rolling Stones' "Satisfaction" which was blaring over the ship's speakers.

I accepted the surprisingly cold Roster's beer they offered and began a stroll through the festivities. I was about halfway around the pool when I saw a woman that stopped me cold. I wasn't sure if she was Asian or not, but I was sure she had the finest pair of legs I'd ever seen. She was wearing white shorts, dark sandals, and a yellow short-sleeved blouse that was knotted at her bare stomach. She had shortish black hair, smooth brown skin, and when she smiled, her cheeks dimpled around bright, white teeth. She was a few inches taller than the local women she was talking to at the far end of the pool.

She must have sensed me looking at her because she lifted her eyes and looked directly at me. The half a second that our eyes locked on each other stunned me.

"AHHH, no-o-o…no!" came a shriek. I turned to look at the source and saw an older Asian lady bouncing up and down and pointing at a small form at the bottom of the pool. Two kids quickly brushed past her and dove into the water. They surfaced seconds later holding a limp body of a small boy above their heads. They kicked their way over to the edge of the pool and handed the child up to the hysterical lady. She clutched him to her chest and wailed harder.

Several bystanders reached out to help her but she jerked away and hugged the body closer to her, bawling even louder. Then the girl that I had just been staring at, pushed through the crowd, stepped up to the panicked woman, and slapped her hard across the face. She said something to the stunned woman in a native tongue then quickly took the child from her.

She laid the small body down and immediately began CPR. Someone thoughtfully turned the music off and things became very quiet. Everyone seemed to be holding their collective breaths, afraid to move or say anything for fear of jeopardizing what the young woman was trying to do. It seemed like minutes passed and the only thing we could hear were breaths of air from the girl. I was beginning to think it was lost cause, when the boy suddenly "*kack, kack*-ed."

The young woman gulped a breath and stared down at the boy.

One of his legs twitched.

"Yeah, yeah, come on, you can do it," somebody urged. More people in several languages offered encouragement as the boy made a gurgling sound. Finally he coughed and began to cry. The lovely girl slid back on her haunches, her face flushed, and smiled up at the crowd. The old woman knelt down and gathered the child in her arms, then reached over and pulled the girl to her. Locked in an embrace, they rocked back and forth. Shouts of joy erupted from the crowd. Looking around I didn't see a dry eye in the house…including mine.

I had forgotten all about wanting to see the rest of the ship. All I wanted to see was the lovely angel that had just performed magic in front of us all. I watched as people crowded around to hug her and shake her hand. Then it struck me; *she's wet and I have a towel! Oh please, don't anybody give her a towel.*

When I finally worked my way next to her, our eyes met again and words failed me. All I could do was take the towel from around my neck and hand it to her.

"Oh yes, thank you," she said in perfect English. She smiled at me while she patted down her arms and neck.

"Thank *you* for what you just did," I finally muttered. I was delighted to hear words coming out of my mouth that seemed to make sense. "I think you just saved a young boy's life. How did you…?"

"Miss Kelli? Excuse me, Miss Kelli?" It was one of the more sober crew members from the ship breaking through the crowd.

"The launch is alongside. We can take you and the boy in if you'd like."

"Oh, yes, we'd better go."

She turned to the child and wrapped my towel around him while speaking to the old lady in dialect. As they gathered themselves to leave she stopped and looked at me. "Oh, I'm sorry, but I think I should go with the boy and his grandma to the hospital, you know, just to make sure…"

"Oh, yes, yes, of course. Go, go," I stammered.

Before stepping off the ship, she looked back at me, smiled, then disappeared.

The jolly soon picked up where it had left off and went on for hours, with our hosts getting drunker and further off key. Mercifully, as it started to get dark, an announcement came over the speakers that the launch was available for those who would like to go ashore.

On the long ride back, I kept thinking about the beautiful girl aboard the tanker. I had to see her again.

CHAPTER FOURTEEN

The next day aboard the *Intrepid*, I stripped down to the uniform of the day, shorts and deck boots, then tackled some projects on deck that needed attention. It was hot, dirty work that needed to be done before we headed back to the States. It was also a weak attempt to keep my mind off the beautiful girl on the tanker.

As the day wore on, I scraped my knuckles and took a shot to my lip when a wrench slipped. I accidentally sprayed hydraulic fluid in my eyes. I tripped over my toolbox and banged a knee. By afternoon I was a sweaty mess and she was still on my mind.

"Hi."

Yeah, that's what her voice sounded like. So soft, like a warm embrace.

"Hello?"

Yes, sweet, just like that.

"Are…are you okay?"

Wha…I jerked my head around. It was her!!

"I hope I'm not bothering you," she said, looking down from the dock directly above me.

"No, no…I was…a…just doin' some chores," I spluttered. "Well, trying to anyway."

She flashed a dazzling smile and said, "It looks like hard work to me."

"It is if you go about it the way I am." I laughed.

There was a pause while my heart pounded away.

"Well—"

"Are you—"

We both laughed then did it again.

"Do you—"

"I was—"

I bowed slightly and said, "No, please, ladies first."

I wasn't sure, but I thought I saw her blush as she pulled a towel out of the plastic bag she was carrying behind her.

I was suddenly feeling very self-conscious standing below this beautiful, long-legged creature. I was dirty, sweaty, and felt I should at least put a shirt on.

"I'm sorry I didn't think to return this to you when we were on the ship," she said, bending over slightly. "Should I toss it down?"

"Oh, yeah, sure…oh, no wait. I'll come up." I hurried into the galley, grabbed a tee-shirt, and hustled up the ladder that was propped up against the mooring. I stepped on the dock, wiping my hands with a rag, and said a little breathlessly, "You didn't have to do this. I'm glad you did though. I mean, I…I didn't need the towel or anything…but I'm, a...I'm glad to see you is what I'm *trying* to say. How's the boy?"

"He's going to be fine. We kept him overnight for observation, but yes, it looks like he'll be okay."

"*We* kept him?"

"I'm a nurse at the hospital here. Well, we call it a hospital anyway; it's pretty small." She laughed. She extended her hand and said, "My name is Kelli, Kelli Jebat."

I went from slowly wiping my hands to frantically trying to get the last of the grease off, and then took her hand in mine. Her hand was warm, slender and felt delicious. *My god, I was feeling like a love-struck schoolboy.*

"Nice to meet you, Kelli. I'm a…Sonny. Sonny Williams."

It occurred to me that I probably should have used an alias, but I wanted this beautiful woman to at least know my name. We stood there and chatted for a while. My nervousness settled somewhat and we both laughed easily together.

"Hey, Sonny, where the fuck did you…?"

Cal had just stepped out the hatch from the galley when he looked up and saw us. "Oh, sorry, I was just looking for the...ah, never mind, I'll find it." He turned and went back inside.

"Sorry 'bout that," I said, turning back to Kelli.

"That's okay." She laughed as she handed me the towel. "Well, I better let you get back to work."

"Oh, yeah, thanks. Ah, say, do you…a…know, do you eat? I mean, of course you eat, what I meant was…" I took a deep breath. "Okay, how do you say in Malay, 'Would you like to meet for lunch sometime soon?'"

She hesitated, smiled, and then said something in a language I didn't understand.

"Well good," I bluffed. "It's settled then. When and where?"

She laughed and said something else I didn't understand and began walking away. I stood there with a stupid grin on my face hoping like hell she was going to say something else, something I *could* understand.

"On second thought," she said as she finally turned around, "better make it the Labuan Hotel restaurant at noon. The food's better there. See you…bye."

Later, back on the boat, Cal asked me about her. "Is that the one you met on the tanker yesterday?"

"Yeah, she brought my towel back. You believe that? She seems really nice. I'm meeting her for lunch tomorrow."

When Cal didn't say anything I began to worry. He was the captain, after all. "That's all right isn't it? I mean, we're not goin' anywhere tomorrow are we?"

"No…no, we're not," Cal said. "In fact, I just found out it'll be at least another week before we head out. Just be careful. Trust no one. Remember, we're just delivering this boat to Singapore if anybody asks."

"Gotcha."

For the first time since this trip began, I wasn't in so much of a hurry to get back.

CHAPTER FIFTEEN

Before noon the next day I must have showered and changed shirts three times, I was sweating like a pig. *Must be this damned tropical heat.* I brushed my hair, looked at myself in the mirror from every angle, and checked for nose strangers. When I realized I wasn't going to get taller or better looking any time soon, I climbed the ladder to the dock and headed for my lunch date.

The restaurant was just off the main lobby of the Labuan Hotel. The restaurant had been intended to double as a nightclub with a bar along one wall and a small adjacent dance floor. There were tables circled around the dance floor and booths along the back wall. Hopes for the success of the place apparently went the way of the oil embargo. It was nearly deserted when I walked in.

There wasn't anybody behind the bar, but I took a seat on a stool anyway. The hint of air-conditioning and the slowly revolving ceiling fans cooled me, but my nerves were on still on high alert.

The last couple of days had gone by in a blur, so I told myself not to be too disappointed if she didn't look as good as I'd remembered.

At noon she walked in and I stopped breathing.

She was stunning.

Her hair. The subtle movement of her blouse. Her shorts. Her legs…damn, *those* legs!

"Hi, Sonny."

Oh Jesus…take a breath…what's her name?! Connie? Carrie?

"Hi, Kelli," I squeaked as I stood to greet her.

She glided towards me and my heart rate kicked up a notch. I caught a hint of a sweet fragrance as she extended her hand.

“Looks like we have our choice of tables.” She laughed and turned to scan the room.

“Or booths” I added, hoping that was her preference. Booths always seemed to be more comfortable and intimate than a table and suddenly I wanted this lovely thing in front of me to be as comfortable and intimate as possible.

“Oh yes, a booth would be fine,” she said as she smiled and waited for me to lead the way.

I picked a booth that was just out of earshot from another couple sitting at a nearby table. As Kelli sat down and scootched herself into the booth, I marveled at her legs once more before they disappeared from view.

I had apparently been too distracted by Kelli’s assets to notice a slender young man had followed us across the room, and I jumped a little when he suddenly spoke.

“Would you like something from the bar before I take your order?” he asked in sing-song English. I noticed his name tag read Ahmad.

Kelli thought a moment, then said, “Just water for me thank you.”

I ordered a beer.

As Ahmad left, Kelli smiled. “Well, how do you like our little island? Or have you been here before?”

She brushed back her hair over one ear I noticed a small, crescent shaped scar, high on her cheek near her left eye. It was more enhancing than distracting.

“No, I’ve never been here,” I answered, “but yes, I like it.” I looked straight into her eyes and added, “The people are very friendly.”

Her smile widened.

The waiter came back with my beer and took our lunch order. We warmed up to each other with polite small talk before she asked more pointedly, “What kind of boat is the *Intrepid*? She doesn’t look like a fishing boat.”

The fact that she referred to the Intrepid as a `she` impressed me. *She must know boats.* I put that away on the back burner of my brain, something I might ask her about later. But for the moment, I was simply struck by the way she cocked her head slightly after asking a question, as if she were truly interested in what I was going to say.

"The *Intrepid* is kind of a work boat…like a tugboat." I said. "She can handle salvage jobs, stuff like that."

"Why are you here?" she asked. My heart skipped a beat.

I smiled. "To have lunch with a pretty girl."

"No," she said and laughed, "you know what I mean!"

I went on to tell her an assortment of lies. I told her that Cal, Bob, Rex and I all worked for a marine delivery service and we were on our way to Singapore to drop off the *Intrepid*. From there we were going to pick up another boat to sail back to the States. I told her we had only stopped at Labuan to make repairs and refuel. I wasn't really comfortable lying to this sweet looking thing so I tried to steer the conversation in another direction. "What about you? Are you a born and raised *Labuanian?*"

I wasn't sure if Labuanian was a word or not but it brought another laugh and smile.

"No, I was born in Singapore. I've only lived here for a few years."

"But you have family here?" I asked.

"No, my mother was born and raised in Singapore and still lives there. My father is an American businessman who travels a lot. I don't have any brothers or sisters. It's just me."

I breathed a little easier and forged ahead. "Well it's probably none of my business, but that means no husband, no boyfriends?"

She blushed before she reached for her water glass and drank what was left. She looked around as if to signal the waiter, but then turned back at me and nodded at my bottle of beer.

"May I?"

"Sure," I said, not sure if she was asking my permission to have a beer or she wanted some of mine.

She answered my question by reaching for the bottle. She took a delicate sip. "Thank you," she said and smiled. The tip of her tongue subtly moistened her lips as she set the bottle down.

I quickly ordered two more beers.

She hadn't answered my question so I tried a different tack, "So why are *you* here?" She took a moment then leaned back and seemed to be considering whether she should tell me or not.

"Well, don't laugh at me, but when I was a little girl, I was fascinated by nurses. Lovely and pristine in their white uniforms. I wanted to be a nurse more than anything. I would set up dolls in my room and pretend they were patients. I can't tell you how many cures for different diseases I discovered! I brought my teddy bear back from the brink of death countless times. I never lost one patient, thank you very much."

She laughed and stopped for a second, her dark brown eyes boring into me. When she saw that I wasn't going to make fun of her, she continued.

"So later when I started college, I found out the school also offered courses in nursing so I signed up. I was hoping that once I graduated, I could see a little more of the world. Singapore was nice enough I guess, but it's a crowded island, and I felt I needed to roam a little. I probably get that from my father." She laughed. "Anyway, when I heard there was a job opening here, I was interested. I didn't even know where Labuan was, I had to look it up!"

"And here you are."

"And here I am."

Our lunch arrived and we turned our attention to it. The sauteed chicken and rice plate I had ordered was delicious, exotic flavors that reminded me of something I couldn't quite place. Kelli had a steaming bowl of soup, which I thought was an odd choice given the tropical locale, but when she cupped one hand under a spoonful and held it over for me to taste, my doubts disappeared. It was superb.

A few more people had wandered in and were scattered around the room having lunch but nobody seemed in a hurry.

I certainly wasn't in a rush to go anywhere. Unfortunately, Kelli had other plans. After finishing her soup, she reached over, took my wrist, and read my watch. "Oh, I didn't realize it was so late. This has been great, but, well, I guess I better go, I still have some things I have to do at the hospital."

My heart sank. "I should get back to the boat as well. Definitely. I've got a lot to do too." I knew she didn't believe me.

As we left the hotel and stepped back into bright sunshine, I fumbled around nervously, going on about how good the food was and how much I enjoyed her company. I sounded like a teenager on his first date. I finally asked if she would like to meet again for lunch again. Sometime. Soon. Like the next day perhaps?

"Oh, I'm sorry, I can't," she said.

Damn. I knew I blew it.

"I have to work a twelve hour shift tomorrow."

"Ah…dinner then?" I knew I was probably sounding desperate but I didn't care. "You know, if you'd like, whenever..."

She hesitated a second, smiled that smile, and said, "I think I'd like that. Can we make it day after tomorrow?"

Can we make it …?Yes! Hallelujah!

"Ah…yeah, sure that's fine. Whatever works for you," I said, shrugging my shoulders. *Stay cool.*

"Do you like Chinese food?"

"Love it," I lied.

We agreed on a time and place and then she said, "Well, thank you for lunch." She extended her hand again, but this time I held on to it a fraction longer than before. She smiled and before I knew it, brushed me with a hug. When she turned and walked away, I slowly sucked in a deep breath, trying to absorb her scent into my skin and lungs for as long as I could.

Cal was the only one aboard when I climbed back on the ship. Bob and Rex had gone ashore to explore a little more of the town.

Cal didn't ask me about my lunch date, thankfully, so I changed into work shorts and spent the afternoon on a couple of jobs in the engine room and puttering around the boat. I tried to concentrate on what I was doing but every time I took a deep breath, Kelli's fragrance danced around and I would replay our lunch in my mind. Other than smiling a lot, I didn't get much accomplished the rest of the day. That evening in the galley, Bob, Rex and I compared notes on where we'd been and what we'd seen of the town so far. We all agreed that the people were friendly and seemed accommodating enough.

"I gotta tell you," Bob said as he patted his belly, "I could get used to this place. They've got those little hibachi thing-a-ma-jigs set up everywhere, cookin` shrimp on just about every corner in town. And they've figured out how to keep the beer cold too. That's pretty much all I need to be happy."

"I don't know," Rex said, "a buck and a half for lunch is a little steep don't you think"? He laughed. "But I did see some nice lookin` women here. Hot women and cold beer! Yeah, can't beat that."

We kicked it around a little bit more, then it grew quiet around the table and I could only think it was because we were all thinking the same thing; *Yeah, the beer and girls are great but let's get this thing finished, let's get home.*

But not before I see Kelli again.

The next morning I had every intention of busying myself with odd jobs. As anybody that has spent time aboard a boat knows, you can always find something to do. Something to tighten, something to loosen, something to paint, something to shine. But whether it was the sun beating down extra hard or my own preoccupation with a certain gorgeous nurse, I had a hard time getting started on anything. The morning passed by grudgingly, like a grandfather clock, tick-tock...tick-tock.

Finally, I gave up on trying to do any real work, but to avoid feeling guilty, I started a list of the things that needed attention. I considered list-making as doing something.

When the sun finally labored it's way up to high noon, we all took a break from whatever we were pretending to do and migrated to the galley. Rex put together some tuna fish sandwiches, and entertained us with stories of his past romantic conquests.

It was a diversion that we let stretch into an hour. Then slowly, one by one, we wandered away in different directions, each of us with our own plan on how to kill the rest of the afternoon. Bob tried a sweaty nap below in the crew's quarters, but soon gave up on it. He surfaced and settled in on the shady side of the wheel house, trying to fashion a hammock out of some old fishing nets he'd found on the dock.

Rex puttered around in the galley, taking inventory and fussing with an electric fan. Cal climbed the ladder to the wheelhouse and rolled out some charts to study until it was time for him to make his afternoon phone call. I went below to tinker in the engine room.

An hour later a shadow filled the hatch above me, and then Cal yelled down, "Hey Sonny, I'm headin` into town, you need anything?"

"Yeah," I shouted back, "if you go by that little hardware store on the corner, see if they have any duct tape, okay?"

"Roger that," he said as his shadow disappeared.

I knew Cal was anxious to get back to sea. He was usually optimistic and in a good mood before he made his phone calls, it was afterward that was a different story.

Then a thought occurred to me and I started to squirm a little; *One day soon he's gonna come back and say "Okay guys, let's roll, were leaving!"*

What would I do? Leave a note at the hospital? "Sorry, had to go, here's my number. If you're ever in Seattle...?"

Do nothing? Just ride away?

An hour and a half later I had my answer. I was on the aft deck when Cal crawled back down the ladder to the *Intrepid*. He tossed me a roll of duct tape and grumbled,"It looks like we're here a while longer." I turned away to hide my smile.

CHAPTER SIXTEEN

The restaurant that Kelli had chosen was at the end of a street two blocks over from the Labuan Hotel and backed up to the jungle. Its steel corrugated roof and cracked stucco matched the rest of the stores and shops in town. Nothing on the outside of the building indicated it was a Chinese restaurant except for a very small sign near the front door that read, "China Seas."

But when I walked inside, it was a different story. There were about twenty tables in the main room, each lighted by red and black Chinese lanterns hanging from the ceiling. Chinese characters, and decorative bunting adorned every wall in the place. Huge porcelain vases stood in the corners of a small waiting area. Waitresses in tight, red, high-collared dresses moved efficiently around the room. Unlike the Labuan Hotel restaurant, the place was nearly full.

Then I spotted Kelli sitting at one of the tables in the far corner of the room. She saw me and waved. As I snaked my way through the tables, I overheard laughter and bits of foreign dialects. I think I was the only Yank in the room and I although I couldn't understand anything being said, I knew laughter well enough and felt very comfortable.

When I neared Kelli's table, again I marveled at her beauty. She was wearing a white Mandarin style blouse with a short collar, unbuttoned nicely at her throat. A thankfully short black skirt swished around her legs as she stood to greet me.

"Hi Sonny, nice to see you again," she said, this time she didn't offer her hand, but floated right into me for a tantalizing hug. It caught me by surprise and before I could stop myself, I kissed her behind her ear. She reacted with a gentle squeeze of my hand.

I liked the way the night was beginning.

Our dinner date went as well as our lunch date if not better. It was exciting to be with Kelli, and at the same time, it felt easy and natural. She was easy to talk to and even easier to listen to. After I told her about growing up in Seattle and how close my brother and I were, she shared some of her childhood memories as well.

"I remember the day my father bought me my first bicycle," she said. "I was so excited I could barely stand it. He was excited too, trotting along side of me, steadying me so I wouldn't fall over. I can still remember how thrilled I was when he finally let me go on my own."

She paused and touched her finger to the scar near her eye, and then with a sheepish smile, added, "Unfortunately, I got a little *too* excited. When I turned to wave at Dad my first solo flight ended…suddenly."

When I began to tell her about my dad and recently losing my mother, she reached for my hand and held it until I finished, her tender brown eyes never leaving mine.

After dinner, Kelli made a marvelous suggestion. "Can we take a walk, down to the water?"

I was only to happy to oblige. We left the restaurant and she led me along a path that wound through some gnarled banyan trees and heavy underbrush. After a short walk we stopped when we came to a clearing and I was able to get my bearings. I could see the Labuan Hotel and beyond that, the harbor. Then I noticed the building that I thought might be the hospital.

"That white building, is that the hospital?" I asked.

"Yes," she answered, "but you're looking at the back of it. The main entrance faces the hotel, more or less."

"And that's where you work?"

"Yep, that's where I work." She paused a second and then smiled, "It's also where I live."

"You *live* at a hospital?!"

"Well, you're close." She laughed, "Come on I'll show you." She slid her arm through mine and off we went.

We walked across a grassy field to a sidewalk that seemed to wrap around around the hospital.

"That's my little apartment," she said, pointing to a cinder block structure that had obviously been an addition to the main building. Five or six circular stepping stones led to a small covered entry.

"Part of the job offer was housing. It's really not bad though, it has everything I need and you can't beat the commute!"

We continued walking around the the building, and I wondered if she was going to show me the inside of her apartment, but when we passed alongside of it, we kept walking along the sidewalk. It eventually took us between the hospital and hotel, and finally to the edge of the harbor. We stood near the shoreline in silence and watched the different colored lights twinkling on the water. Finally I asked her, "If I waded out there in the water, and started to drown, would you administer CPR on me...you know, like you did for that young boy on the tanker?"

She looked into my eyes. "Even though that was the worst pick-up line I've ever heard, there's just something about you..." She smiled and slid into my arms. Her kiss was gentle at first, and then we got hungry. When we came up for air, she breathed into my ear, "Maybe we should head back toward the hospital, Sailor, you know, as a precaution. I...I may need to keep you awhile for observation."

"I think that's a good idea, Nurse. I'm pretty sure I have a temperature."

CHAPTER SEVENTEEN

I don't know what time it was when I crawled back aboard the *Intrepid*, but I slept better than I had in a long time. When I did wake up, I had the strength and attitude of a contented noodle. I skipped a morning shower, not willing to wash away the scent of the previous night just yet and whistled my way to the galley. The rest of the crew was already there.

"Hey Rex, how's it goin`?"

"Wha...?"

"Hi Bob, how's the coffee?"

"What are you smilin` about?"

"Mornin`Cal."

"Fuck you Williams."

I grabbed my cup of coffee and sat down, joining Cal and Bob at the salon table. Rex shuffled over and shoved a plate with some toast on it in my direction then went back to work at the stove.

During my navy days it was almost a requirement that you shared details about your time ashore with your shipmates, especially if there was a woman involved. But I didn't think my time with Kelli was a kiss-and-tell kinda thing.

This was too much for Rex. After a minute or two he came back to the table, slid two eggs on my plate and stood there, looking at me. "Well? How was it?"

"The toast? Oh it was burnt a little, but…"

"Don't give me that shit. You know, last night?"

"Oh, last night. Yeah, it was…nice."

Rex looked astonished and stood there, frying pan and spatula in hand.

"*Nice?* That's all you got for me?...Nice?!"

When I just smiled, he gave it another second, turned and went back to his stove, muttering the entire time. "Well shit, I guess I'm gonna have to go to town tonight myself. Nice?...What the fuck is that?"

I spent the morning and early afternoon in just shorts and work boots, breezing through the work list I'd made the day before. Replays of the night with Kelli would drift in and out of my mind and leave me smiling. I really wanted to see her again as soon as possible but I wasn't sure how to go about it. I knew she was working a late shift at the hospital but I thought if I just showed up on her doorstep, I might be pushing it. Better to back off a little for now.

By two o'clock, I was done with the last item on my work list and was on the aft deck cleaning my tools, and watching some birds making a fuss, squawking and diving into the water about twenty yards away. Some of the birds came up gargling small fish; some came up with empty beaks and just blinked.

Then I noticed a small boy running down the dock. When he reached the *Intrepid* he slowed to a walk and looked down at me. The tide was out and I was probably standing fifteen feet below him.

"Mr. Sonny? He asked. He had a small white envelope in his hand.

"Yeah, that's me."

"Miss Kelli say give you this, okay?"

"Yeah, sure, I'll..."

Before I could stop him, he wound up, threw the envelope in my direction and then took off running back the way he'd come. The envelope fluttered like a butterfly, first one way, then the other. I watched it twitching it's way down to me but just before I could reach up and grab it, it flirted away, toward the dock and over the side. I took a quick step to the gunwale and saw it floating under the dock near a piling. I spun around and looked for something to snag it with, Bob's fishing net, a gaff, anything! Finding nothing and realizing I had already wasted precious seconds, I kicked off my boots and dove over the side.

My wake pushed the envelope a little farther under the dock, but with one stroke, I was able to reach it and grab it with my left hand. Holding it above my head, I instinctively kicked and sidestroked my way back to the *Intrepid.* That's when I realized climbing back aboard wasn't an option. Since we hadn't refueled yet, the boat was riding so high out of the water, I couldn't reach the tires that hung down along the sides. I turned and kicked my way to the steel ladder that was attached to the dock. I grabbed a rung and hung there, coughing and catching my breath.

"Should I be concerned about anything Williams?"

I looked up to see Cal leaning over the top rail just outside the bridge. He had one foot on the lower rail and a cigar in his right hand.

"Nah, everything's cool. Just rescuing some air mail here," I looked away and waved the envelope over my head, feeling a little foolish.

I climbed up a few rungs and when I looked up again, Cal was gone.

I was almost dry by the time I stepped back aboard the *Intrepid.* The steel deck was much too hot to stand on barefoot and I jumped around like a fart in a skillet before I found my boots and pulled them on. After flicking off what water I could from the envelope, I carefully opened it. I felt like a kid with his first Valentine's day card.

I unfolded the paper inside and immediately saw that some of the ink was blurred, but I could read most of it: "Sonny, Thank yo...uch fo last night I h...on... I th...you ar...n. I h.... to work tonig...bu....`ve got ...or...off. ould you like to see the rest of the islan...morrow? Com...in the morn...if you ca...K."

I could read just enough to decipher the invitation to come by her apartment in the morning. That was enough for me.

But I knew I'd better check with Cal before I planned anything with Kelli. He also had to be a little curious as to what was in an envelope worth jumping overboard for, so I headed to the wheelhouse and showed him the note.

"She can't spell worth a shit, can she?" He handed back the note and said with a smile, "Maybe you better go see her tomorrow, find out what the hell she's talking about."

CHAPTER EIGHTEEN

Before leaving the Intrepid the next day, I caught up with Cal to see if he needed me for anything.

"Yeah, I'm thinking we might as well put in our order for fuel," he said. "It'll give us something to do besides sitting here on our asses. Besides, once we refuel, it'll be easier for you to get back aboard if you decide to go diving for envelopes again."

"So, you want me to stay on the boat?"

"Nah, it'll probably take a couple of days for the shipyard to get their act together once I put the order in, I just need an estimate of how much fuel to order. You mind dipping the tanks before you go?"

"No need to Skip, I can tell you right now how much fuel we'll need."

I waited for him to get something to write on, then rattled the numbers. When he finished writing he looked at me and said, "Well okay then, I'll see you later. Don't get shanghaied or nothin`. Remember what we're doing here."

On the way to Kelli's I thought about what Cal had said. He had a good point.

What am *I doing here? I met a beautiful girl. So what?*

I got lucky last night. Big deal. If I play my cards right I might get a repeat performance before we leave.

But we are leaving.

Remember that.

I was three steps away from Kelli's porch when she opened the door. Any thoughts of making sense of anything, or being noble, disappeared in a flash when I saw her. She was barefoot in white short-shorts, a tank top, and was briskly toweling her hair. Her breasts danced invitingly.

Remember what you're doing here.

"Hi Sonny, I guess you got my message?" she asked with a smile.

"Huh...? Oh, yeah. Well sort of, I couldn't read it all."

She gave me a funny look as she motioned me inside, still drying her hair. When I unfolded the note to show her, I noticed the paper was even more worse for wear, probably due to some last minute sweating on my part.

"Oh no, what happened?"

When I told her, she covered her mouth and began laughing. When she finally regained her composure, she reached for my hand."Oh Sonny, I'm sorry, I don't mean to laugh, but I can just see you..."

I pulled her to me and kissed her before she could say anything more. I felt a desire surge through me, an intensity that I'm not sure I've ever experienced at eight o'clock in the morning. When we finally broke apart she said breathlessly, "Well, good morning to you too. Does this mean you *can* spend the day with me?"

"Do we have to leave your apartment?" I asked and went back for a quick nibble behind her ear.

"You funny man, Yankee," she said in a playful Chinese accent. Then she pushed me back and asked, "Can I take you sailing, sailor?"

"You can take me anywhere you want young lady. How about right here on the kitchen floor?"

"Hmm," she said, tracing my lips with her finger. "I do have a futon, and with some pillows...?"

She pretended to give it some thought then tossed her hair back and said, "Nope, sorry, it's too beautiful outside. I thought you'd like to see more of our island? There's a tiny marina on the windward side where I have a small boat. My father taught me how to sail when I was a kid, and I'd love to take you out. It's much cooler there. It's where I go to relax."

"Sounds great. My second favorite thing to do is relax."

CHAPTER NINETEEN

The island of Labuan was small, but it did have an airport. It was located in the middle of the island and was serviced by a couple of small taxis, or jeepneys that shuttled people back and forth from town. For a few U.S. dollars, or Malaysian ringgit, you could hire a jeepney driver to take you anywhere you wanted to go on the island.

With a cooler full of beer and good things to eat, Kelli and I settled into the back seat of an open air jeepney piloted by a good-natured man named Hector. We were soon headed for the other side of the island. Hector was a short, well built man, with very dark skin and a full head of black curly hair. When he smiled he exposed an expanse of white teeth set off by a single gold tooth in front. Five miles out of town, Hector asked over his shoulder. "You wan go short cut, see jungle maybe?"

Kelli started to say something but I cut her off and said, "Sure why not?" A split second after the words left my mouth, Hector yanked the wheel to the right and soon we were bouncing and twisting our way through thick foliage and over what passed as a road. If there was anything of interest to see, I sure as hell couldn't focus on it, my eyeballs were bouncing around like pinballs.

Twenty minutes later, trailing a hundred yards of dust, the road suddenly flattened out and we came to a stop. As the dust settled around us, I heard the plane before I saw it; it was a faint buzz at first, then it seemed to grow louder. I was straining to see where it was coming from when an unexpected breeze cleared the air. Suddenly I was looking at a twin-engine, turbo prop airplane barreling down a runway straight at us.

"Dis airport, main building over der," Hector said, pointing in tourist guide fashion. He nonchalantly put the jeep in gear and said, "Nex stop, marina." We cleared the runway just as the plane cleared us.

If my loins were stirred earlier, they were now completely shaken.

Eventually Hector found a gravel road that led out to a point on the island. The palm trees that lined the road fluttered in the breeze, indicating we were indeed on the windward side of the island. As we drew closer, I could see a small wooden shack sitting off to the side of a pier that jutted out into a small bay. An old Coca-Cola sign dangled off one side of the tiny building, rattling in the breeze. There were three small sailboats in their berths, four if you counted the one that was submerged, it's mast defiantly sticking straight up out of the water.

As we crunched to a stop on the gravel, a dark-skinned old man emerged from the shack, a scrawny dog in step behind him. He adjusted a wide-brimmed straw hat and smiled. He said something in the local dialect to Hector, and then turned to us; "Nice to see you too Miss Kelli. You takin` *Jewel* out today?"

"Yes Mohammed, I am. And it's good to see you as well. I'd like you to meet my friend, Sonny."

As Kelli made introductions, Hector carried our cooler down and set it in front of the boat that was in the slip farthest away from us. We were still talking with the old man when Hector returned to his jeep and said,"When you wan me back?"

Kelli looked at me, but I just shrugged. It was her call.

"Better make it about seven if you can," she said.

"Tonight?" he asked..

"Yes, of course tonight. I have to be at work early tomorrow!" Kelli laughed, and then looked back at me. "The boat does have a small cabin, but it's too tiny for sleepovers"

"Okay-dokay, seven o'clock," Hector said as he climbed into his jeep.

As we turned to go down the dock, Kelli took my hand and breathed into my ear, "Don't worry, there's a nice secluded beach just in case we need to lie down for any reason."

The boat Kelli called *Jewel* looked to be about twenty-four feet long with a small cuddy cabin just aft of a single mast. A wooden tiller bisected the cockpit and its two bench seats. The boat was made from fiberglass with dark mahogany trim and handrails. Unlike the other boats around her, she looked well-kept.

Shortly after we pushed away from the dock, Kelli assigned me to the tiller while she opened the door to the cuddy-cabin and wrestled out a rolled up sail. She tossed the sail forward over the cabin, then hopped up and started snapping things in place. In only a moment or two she began raising the mainsail. There was a nice tropical breeze at our backs and as Kelli worked the sail up the mast, I felt the boat begin to move.

Kelli knelt on the deck and watched the sail for a minute, and then stuck her head back into the cabin. Soon she had another rolled up sail over her shoulder that she treated the same way as the first one, pitching it forward over the cabin.

"You're doing a good job `tiller-man`, she said. "Just keep her headed like that and I'll go forward and put up the jib."

As I sat in the small cockpit with one hand on the tiller, I realized I didn't know a hell of a lot about sailing, but I did know I enjoyed the hell out of watching Kelli go about her business. She moved around the boat like a cat, her delicate calf and thigh muscles defining themselves with each barefoot step. Watching as she stretched her supple body to make adjustments in the sails, I nearly forgot what I was doing at the helm.

"Hey Matey, keep her into the wind or it's forty lashes for you!" Kelli yelled back at me as the sails began to luff.

I quickly moved the tiller and the sails filled again.

"Hmm, forty lashes? You promise?"

Kelli gave me a come hither look that almost made me forget the tiller again.

It didn't take us long to find the right balance between sail and helm and we were soon scooting over the water as if we had someplace to go.

I learned to duck at the right times when Kelli called for a change in directions and enjoyed the occasional spray of salt water on my face. At one point Kelli playfully sat on my lap while she handled the sheets, sometimes pulling the lines in, sometimes playing them out as we made long runs on open water. I could feel her taut body working through my thighs and I loved every minute of it. She was quite good at handling her boat and I could tell she was happy on the water.

I was just as happy, at least I was until I saw a giant dorsal fin sticking straight out of the water about thirty feet in front of us. An even taller tail fin in the shape of a scythe trailed ten feet behind it. Kelli spotted the same thing at almost the same time. "Sonny! Look! A whale shark! Isn't it beautiful? Quick, head us into the wind, I'll get the sails down."

Excuse me? Get the sails...down?

When I didn't respond, she looked back at me, smiling excitingly. "Don't worry, whale sharks don't bother humans. They just swim along with their mouths open, feeding on plankton and sucking in whatever is in front of them. If they take in the wrong thing, they just flush it out their gills. Do you always get this nervous around animals a hundred times your size?" She winked at me. "They're just big ol` gentle giants really."

I followed orders but with some consternation. I could see the beast was at least ten feet *longer* than the *Jewel* so there was no question about it being a giant; it was the gentle part I wasn't so sure about.

As we drew closer I could see the creature had a wide, flattened head and a blunt nose. It's head moved continuously from side to side in a slow languid motion and I could see white spots all along its massive, grayish colored back. A few small fish swam nonchalantly in front of its gaping mouth. It reminded me of those old Jacques Cousteau television specials where you'd see a diver hang on to the big fish's back and hitch a ride.

Not this cowboy.

We watched it move around our boat for five or six minutes, and then as if it were waving goodbye, it gave a couple of easy wags with its enormous tail and slipped away.

Neither of us said anything for a moment. Kelli put her arm around my waist and whispered,"Wow, that was something wasn't it?"

"Yes it was." I paused for a moment then added, "And you know what? Watching it feeding like that has made me hungry. You *did* say something about a secluded beach nearby, did you not? Let's have a picnic. All the plankton you want, my dear"

"Throw in a cold beer or two, and I'm there," Kelli said as she kissed my shoulder. "I'll go start the engines."

The landing site Kelli had picked out was definitely secluded. As we approached the shoreline I could see nothing but empty beaches on either side of a horseshoe-shaped cove. Small waves splashed large rocks that stood guard on each side of the entrance. The water in the cove was an emerald green and fronted a white sandy beach. Palm trees lined the sand, waving at us, inviting us ashore.

Because *Jewel* was outfitted with a center board keel system that we could raise or lower, we were able to sail her well into the cove before anchoring in less than three feet of water.

Our plan called for wading ashore and I knew Kelli had thought to put on a two piece bathing suit under her shorts and tank top, but still it thrilled me when she stood in the cockpit and wiggled out of her shorts, then pulled her tank top over her head. She caught me looking at her and stuck out her tongue. I laughed as I balanced the cooler on the starboard gunwale, then eased myself overboard and pulled the cooler with me. Kelli stacked a couple of towels on her head and followed behind. We were soon ashore and I let Kelli lead the way. I enjoyed the view.

"Do you like it here?" Kelli said, spreading out one of the towels at the base of a palm tree.

"Well, let's see," I said as I opened two beers, "The weather is perfect, the scenery is gorgeous, and there are no other humans around. I'm with a beautiful, exotic female that knows how to sail and likes beer! I'm not sure."

Kelli took the beer I offered and then with her free hand, hooked two fingers in the waist band of my shorts and tugged me toward her. "I'm not sure about that beautiful, exotic stuff, but I do know, that *I* like it here…with you."

We started nuzzling each other, but my stomach rudely interrupted us with a gurgling growl.

Kelli laughed. "I need to feed you! We better eat!"

"Mmm...I know what I'm hungry for, and it's not food."

"You have a one track mind, sir."

I sat crossed legged on the towels, taking the last bite of my sandwich. I was about to finish off another beer, when Kelli leaned over with a bottle of lotion, and asked a silly question. "Would you like me to rub some oil on your back? A massage for dessert?"

Without saying a word, I put my beer on the ground and flipped over on my stomach.

Kelli laughed, "I guess that means yes."

I felt Kelli straddle me as a couple of drops of lotion hit my back. I heard a cap being screwed back on then felt Kelli's warm, soft hands begin their magic.

Did I like it here? What a silly woman.

We spent the rest of the afternoon making love in the shade, and when it moved, we made love in the sun. We ate again and napped. We walked on the beach, then waded out into the shallow water. We stopped and held each other. Kelli looked at me seductively, licked her lips, and then began moving her head easily from side to side, doing her best imitation of a whale shark. Slowly she lowered herself in front of me.

The *Jewel* sat nearby, her nose pointed seaward, nodding approvingly.

Hours later, when the sun starting to dip below the tops of the palm trees, we loaded our supplies back aboard the *Jewel* and slowly sailed out of our hidden paradise.

"Kinda hard to leave isn't it?" Kelli asked as we stood together in the cockpit. I answered by lifting the hair from the back of her neck and kissing her there. We were in no hurry to get back to any kind of civilization.

Kelli didn't bother with the jib and sat with me at the tiller. Contentedly, we rode the *Jewel* back to the marina.

Hector was waiting on the dock as we eased back into our slip. The old man and dog were nowhere to be seen.

"Good to see you my friends," Hector said as he helped secure the boat. "You have good time, yes?"

Kelli and I just looked at each other and grinned.

"Okay-dokay then," he said, quickly grabbing the empty cooler and towels and hustling back to his jeep to wait for us.

When Kelli and I eventually caught up to him and climbed in the back, he smiled and said, "Long way home maybe, yes?"

❧

The ride back to town was peaceful and it was almost dark when Hector dropped us off at Kelli's apartment.

We said our good nights on the porch….or at least we tried to.

With her back to the door, Kelli reached up and touched my cheek. "Thank you so much for today."

I took her hand and kissed it. "No, thank *you*."

We stared at each for a minute, and then I said, "I'd go sailing with you anytime. You run a tight ship, but you know what you're doing!"

"Do I?" she asked as she leaned in and kissed me.

We stayed in the kiss longer than we should have and before I knew it, I was in lock-step with Kelli as she walked backward, pulling me into her apartment.

An hour later, I smacked Kelli with a pillow, said goodnight, and picked myself off the kitchen floor.

CHAPTER TWENTY

When you enlist in The U.S. Navy, you're issued a uniform and a book of rules and regulations known as the Bluejackets Manual. In that manual you can find everything you need to know about how to wear the uniform, certain protocol, chain of command, and what was expected of you as a sailor.

Aboard the *Intrepid*, we didn't have a manual; shorts was the uniform of choice with shirts optional, and our chain of command started and stopped with Cal. After that, the only thing we had was an unwritten rule that we all get up in the morning no matter what you did the night before. When Rex served breakfast the next morning, I could tell he wasn't in the best of shape.

"Morning Rex."

"What? Oh yeah...you want eggs or somethin`?"

I decided to make it easy on him."Nah, I'm just gonna have some toast and coffee."

I could hear Cal above us in the wheelhouse, swearing and muttering to himself about radio frequencies.

"Don't work Rex too hard this morning Sonny," Bob said over his cup of coffee. "He had a rough night last night."

"I did *no*t have a rough night last night," Rex countered, "in fact if they hadn't closed the bar so early, I would've scored with the waitress. You were there, you saw how she was lookin` at me!"

"Yeah, I remember *exactly* how she was lookin` at you." I glanced at Bob and he had his eyes crossed and his tongue hanging out.

"I'm just not having as much fun feeding you fuck-heads right now," Rex said as he turned back to his stove.

I was pouring myself a second cup when we all heard Cal roar from the wheelhouse above, "Goddamn it! I *am* transmitting on that frequency you stupid shit!" Two seconds later, he rumbled down the ladder, grabbed a coffee cup and stuck it under the pot I held in my hand. "Why is it so *god*- damn hard to get anything done around here?!"

"What's up Cal? Whadda you want us to do?" One of the things I liked about Bob was his confident, easy going manner which usually had a calming effect. It certainly worked on Cal.

"Ah, it's okay, nothin` you can do." Cal said, backing off a bit. "I was just trying to call the shipyard to confirm our fuel order. I phoned them yesterday and they said to call `em back today on the radio and they'd tell us when to move the boat over to the fuel dock. I probably heard `em wrong or somethin`. I'll go into a town a little later and call `em again. I might as well make my other call while I'm there. See if we're ever gonna get outta here."

"When you goin`?" Bob asked. "I think I should go back to the hotel. We may have left a tab there last night."

"Tab? We didn't leave a tab there last night." Rex interrupted. "I'm sure we paid...wait, when you goin'?"

"I'm goin` in about an hour." Cal said.

Bob nodded. "I'll go with you."

Cal and Bob both turned and looked at Rex, waiting for him to say something.

"Ah, well, you guys go ahead. I better stay here...but, ah...if you get a chance to duck into the hotel bar, see if that same girl is workin` tonight, would you?"

After Cal and Bob headed for town I realized I was a little disappointed that nobody asked me about my day on the other side of the island. I supposed they thought I'd just tell `em it was nice again, but this time I was a little more willing to open up a bit. I knew I wouldn't be comfortable sharing the intimate details, but I wanted to tell someone how much fun I had sailing with such an exquisite woman, seeing a whale shark, settling under a palm tree in a secluded part of paradise and having...lunch.

Then I thought about Tim. He would be the one person that would really appreciate the day. I thought about calling him but I knew he'd want to know when we were leaving. Since I didn't know that yet, I decided to wait until I did.

I didn't have to wait long.

I was in the wheelhouse looking through binoculars at the shipyard across the bay, trying to spot anything that resembled a fuel dock when Cal and Bob came back from town. I heard Cal whistling his way into the galley below, and thought about an ancient superstition many old salts had about whistling aboard a ship; it was bad luck. As far as beliefs went, whistling on a working boat was right up there with sailing out of port on a Friday, or having a woman aboard.

I slid down the ladder to the galley and joined Cal and Bob at the settee. From the look on Cal`s face, I knew something was up.

"Well, is she working tonight?" Rex asked, stepping through the aft hatch.

"What? Oh that, I forgot. Sorry," Cal answered, "But I've got good news. We just got our marching orders."

"The load's ready? We're leaving?" Rex asked.

"That's right. Soon as we fuel up, we can leave anytime."

"You get a hold of the shipyard?" I asked, trying to bring things into focus.

"Yep. They'll be ready for us tonight."

Nobody said anything for a moment or two, and then Cal laid out the rest of the plan.

"We'll move over to the fuel dock at four-thirty. While we're refueling, one of the shipyards` cranes will set six, fifty gallon drums of oil, and two drums of gasoline on deck, port side."

Cal stopped to look at me. “That’s what we need, right Williams?”

I just nodded my head, still digesting the news.

“We’ll spend the night at the shipyard and make any last minute repairs there. In the morning we’ll move back here, take on fresh fruits and that sorta stuff and top off our fresh water tanks just before leave. That work for you Rex?”

Rex answered the same way I did.

“Our rendezvous point is fifty miles off the southern tip of Viet Nam. I figure it’ll take us three days to get there, weather permitting. We still didn’t know how big the load is or how many boats will be meeting us, so we’ll have to play those things by ear.”

Cal took a slug of coffee and waited for someone to say something. When nobody did he continued.

“Okay, once we’re loaded, we’ll head up through the South China Sea then take a right when we make the Pacific. After that, it’s pretty much what we’ve already talked about. We’ll off-load approximately six hundred miles from San Francisco. Once we’re off-loaded, we head for Ensenada, Mexico. From there, we’ll tie up the boat, walk away from it, then make our way back across the border.”

“And live happily ever after.” Rex chuckled.

“And live happily ever after,” echoed Cal. Then he said something that surprised me. “But since we’re gonna be at sea for another month or more, I’m thinkin` we should have a little fun before we leave here. I know you guys probably wanna say goodbye to some of the folks here, so whadda you say we make a day of it? We could invite some of the people from the hotel and take them out to that deserted island,‘Sleeping Lady’ I think the locals call it, and have a jolly ourselves. We could anchor in close and take the Zodiac ashore, full of beer of course.”

“When you thinkin`?” Bob asked.

“Well, we don’t have much time.” Cal shrugged, “If you guys wanna do this, we better do it tomorrow. I figure around ten o’clock.”

"Hell yes let's do it," Rex chimed in. "I'll get what's-her-name to go!"

"You mean the barmaid that's crazy about you?" asked Bob.

"Yeah, that's the one," Rex said without missing a beat. "And Sonny can bring his sweet potato. She's probably got some friends that`d wanna come, right Sonny?"

My head was spinning. "Ah, yeah, sure. I'll ask."

I had been wondering how I was going to say goodbye to Kelli when it came time to leave. Maybe this was as good a way as any.

"Okay, we'll do it," Cal said."I'll see if that guy at the hardware store wants to come."

Cal`s words hung in the air and nobody said anything for a few heart beats. Bob raised his eyebrows up and down and elbowed Rex. And then Cal noticed the expression on our faces. "His *sister*, assholes! He'll bring his sister!"

While the rest of the crew of the *Intrepid* happily put their guest list together, I started scribbling a note to Kelli.

`*We have to take the boat over to the shipyard tonight, but we'll be back tomorrow. Cal thinks we should have a jolly aboard the Intrepid when we get back, maybe go out to Sleeping Lady around ten. It's not quite sailing aboard the Jewel, but what could be? Invite a couple of your friends if you want, they can create a distraction for us.*

See you in the morning …?

Sonny`

Cal and the boys were still jawing about who should come along on our jolly when I left the *Intrepid* and headed into town. I thought about going to the hospital to see if I could talk with Kelli, but I knew if I was going to have time to call Tim, I better just drop the note off at Kelli`s apartment and get on with my business.

After wedging the note in the door, I hustled over to the Labuan Hotel and placed my call to Seattle.

"Hello?" Tim sounded awake this time.

"Hey now, how you doin`?"

"Hey, I'm alright! You okay?"

"Yeah, I'm fine, everything's good here. In fact we're getting ready to leave."

"Yeah? Cool! Everything's okay then? I've been worried sick."

"Oh yeah, we had a bit of a delay, but now it's all systems go."

"Man that's good to hear. Everything's all right then huh?"

"Hey," I said and laughed, "how many times I gotta tell you, everything's fine."

"Okay, okay….so, when you think you'll be home? Or you know, back on this side of the planet?"

"Well, we're gonna have a jolly tomorrow, than get under way right after that, so…."

"You're gonna have a what?"

"Oh, a jolly. A party on the boat. Hey, I met a gal I think you'd like, she's…."

Suddenly, all I could hear was static, then, "…. what? A party?….what's going on? Who's…."

Our connection started to deteriorate, and I could hear Tim talking but couldn't make out what he was saying.

"What? I'm losing you, I can't hear you." I said. After a few more moments of crackling I said, "If you can hear me, well, I'll...I'll see you soon, okay?"

I listened to static for another minute, then hung up.

CHAPTER TWENTY-ONE

We spent a long night at the shipyard, but got everything we needed. The oil and fuel drums were secured along the port rail and for the first time in about six weeks, the *Intrepid* was socked down with fuel and riding low in the water. I checked all the fluid levels in everything that needed checking and cleaned the filters in the generators and air compressors. It felt good to be sweating and working. I knew I needed to keep my mind on what I was doing, but as much as I tried, I couldn't help worrying that Kelli didn't get my message or that she couldn't get away. The phone call to Tim bothered me too, although I wasn't sure why.

At eight o'clock the next morning we shoved off and headed back across the bay. Cal, Bob and Rex were all in a good mood, obviously looking forward to the day ahead, but also to getting back to sea and taking care of business. I wasn't sure if I was nervous, excited, worried, or all three, but the mood had definitely changed aboard the *Intrepid*.

We were all gathered in the wheelhouse as we approached the pier and were surprised to see it was virtually empty of vessels. Apparently most of the ships that had been tied up alongside of us had left during the night. Cal had been getting better at handling the boat but I think he was relieved to see it would be an easy approach to the dock. We could also see a small group of people gathered near a cleat at the far end of the pier and Cal put the glasses on them. "My God, it looks like there's about eight or nine people standing there. You don't suppose they're waiting for us do you? I told `em ten o'clock!"

"Well, these people are like the Chinese," Bob said. "They consider it rude to decline an invitation. They lose face if they do."

"Let me see those glasses," Rex said to Cal. He spent a second or two adjusting the lenses. "Hey, I think she's there! Yeah, I think that's her!" Rex put the glasses down and glanced at Bob. "Hey, you mean if I invite her to sleep with me, she'd have to accept?"

"No, it doesn't works that way. You'll have to use that sexy-Rexy charm of yours."

"No problem then."

I took the binoculars from Rex and did my own survey of the people on the dock. I recognized a couple of them from the hotel, but there was no Kelli.

We throttled back as we got closer, then like a plane coming in low over a runway, we made a shallow approach to the dock and glided along the length of the pier, finally nudging in alongside the group of people.

Bob was on the bow ready to toss a hawser to a cleat when Cal stepped outside the wheelhouse. "Morning Mr. Jhan," Cal shouted, spotting the tiny man from the hardware store. "You mind catching a line for us?"

The tide was up so it wouldn't be much of a toss, and I knew Cal was just doing it as an act of courtesy to involve our guest. Mr. Jhan gleefully clapped his hands and Bob heaved the line toward him, unfortunately hitting Mr. Jhan in the face, knocking his hat and glasses sideways on his head. Bob immediately jumped to the dock to help, but Mr. Jhan recovered quickly. Without bothering to straighten his hat or glasses, he flipped the loop of the line over the cleat like a cowboy roping a calf and then proudly looked up at Cal.

"Perfect! Good job", Cal yelled, and gave the shopkeeper a thumbs-up. "And I see your sister was able to come. That's great."

Standing next to Mr. Jhan was a very pretty girl in a summery dress and a wide brimmed hat, smiling brightly. I think Cal`s smile was even bigger.

I spent the next twenty minutes welcoming our guests aboard and playing tour guide. Along with Mr. Jhann and his sister, there was Ahmad, the bartender from the hotel; the waitress that Rex was hot for and a couple of her girl friends. There was also another man and woman that I remembered from a corner food stand.

As I was showing everyone around the boat, the thought crossed my mind that maybe this wasn't such a good idea. I wasn't sure the old man would approve of me being a tour guide aboard his boat.

"*....and this is where we'll be stowing the marijuana. We'll have to dismantle the bunks in the sleeping quarters of course, as we're expecting anywhere from ten to twenty tons of premium Thai weed. Over here is where we keep our weapons....*"

I was getting even more nervous with each glance at my watch and still no Kelli, when Bob yelled to me from outside the bridge, "Hey Sonny, is that your sweet thing?"

He was pointing to three more people coming down the dock.

Kelli was laughing with another girl and walking ahead of a sailor I remembered from the tanker jolly. His name was Sebastian and he was pushing a cart with scuba gear and had a guitar strapped to his back.

The first thing Kelli did when she came aboard was offer me her hand. The gesture still thrilled me, and I pulled her to me and gave her a quick nuzzle behind her ear.

Blushing slightly Kelli introduced me to her friend. "Sonny, this is my friend, Liala. Her family owns a market in town."

"Nice to meet you Liala," I said and bowed slightly.

Liala was no bigger than a minute with large brown eyes and an even bigger smile. “Nice to meet you Mr. Sonny. Kelli tell me ‘bout you,” she giggled.

Kelli shrugged her shoulders and grinned, “What can I say? You’re a charmer, sailor.”

A few minutes later, Cal counted heads and decided that eleven passengers were enough for our little party, so we cast off and swung the *Intrepid* seaward. As we moved toward open water, I thought about the huge tanker that had hoisted the original jolly, it was almost ten times longer than the *Intrepid* and had about ten times as many guests. But I didn’t care. There was only one guest that interested me.

The day was perfect. A few high puffy clouds floated above a light breeze that kept the tropical heat reasonable. Some guests mingled around the boat as we cruised along at half speed; others were content to stand along the rail in the shade of *Intrepid`s* cabin, chatting and enjoying themselves.

It wasn’t long before one of our guests pointed to an island on the horizon. The island looked to be about two or three miles long. Without using too much imagination you could see the form of a woman lying on her back, breasts jutting straight up. Sleeping Lady could just as easily be called, “Nice Boobs” island.

Thirty minutes later we slowed as we neared the lee side of the island looking for a good place to anchor. The island was beautiful with palm trees lining brilliant white sandy beaches. The shoreline twisted and turned, forming lagoons of crystal clear water. It was hard to believe there weren’t any other people around.

Finally we agreed on a spot and dropped the hook. We quickly loaded a couple of the coolers and some of the guests into the Zodiac and I ferried them ashore, leaving them to set up shop. I hurried back for the rest of the people and their gear and within twenty minutes we were all ashore.

Rex and Cal carried one of the heavier coolers up the beach to a grassy, shady spot, while Ahmad followed behind with a smaller cooler and a large bag that he had brought with him. As soon as Rex and Cal sat their burden down, Ahmad began to fuss and straighten things out like he was assuming the role of bartender, although Cal instructed him otherwise. "You don't have to serve us, Ahmad, we can get our own beer."

"I understand Captain," Ahmad said as he pulled some plastic cups out of his bag, "but if you prefer something else, I would be most happy to serve you." He smiled and pulled out a bottle of rum, followed by a bottle of gin, then one of vodka.

Bob helped Sebastian lug the scuba gear up the beach where they began inspecting the equipment. Kelli and Liala spread towels out under a palm tree and my mind flashed back to a recent similar scene that starred just me and Kelli. I desperately wanted to be alone with Kelli and figured at some point I would be. I *had* to be.

"Hey Sonny!, you wanna take a dive?" Bob yelled at me, flapping a swim fin in the air. I looked over at Kelli. She smiled and waved at me to go ahead.

"Splendid day for a dive 'eh mates?" Sebastian said as we all helped each other into our gear. He was a friendly enough guy, tall and lanky with a black bushy mustache and fortunately, wasn't as drunk as I remembered him being on the tanker. Once we had our gear strapped on, we gave each other a thumbs-up and soon the three of us were walking backward into the sea.

I had only been scuba diving a few times and with all the gear on, I felt clumsy above the surface, but once submerged, it was a different story. With Sebastian leading the way, we slowly descended into the crystal clear water, swimming easily and enjoying every minute of it.

Fish of every description darted in front of us, some stopping to look straight on at the bubbling invaders, others languidly moving off into the far shadows. We explored the outer reaches of the lagoon then swam back along the ocean bottom, weaving our way through long, vertical strands of brown seaweed.

As the sea floor gradually took us up toward the beach, Bob tapped me on the shoulder and pointed forward and toward the surface. Two swimmers were above us. One had the legs of a girl; the others` legs were scrawny, like...Rex`s? Even underwater, I could see the twinkle in Bob's eyes and knew exactly what he had in mind. I gave him a thumbs up and we both moved stealthy upwards, toward the dangling feet.

Two hours later, sitting around the beach, people were still laughing and kidding Rex about the "shark attack."

"Why you swim away so fast?" one of the gals teased him. "You scream like girl."

"Hey, I knew they were there." Rex said weakly. "I, ah...I could see their bubbles...I was just playing along."

Sebastian, who had been strumming his guitar, immediately broke into an impromptu version of, "Tiny Bubbles." Mr. Jhann who was on his third or fourth beer joined in on the second verse, which got everybody laughing and singing along. Finally Rex took a big swig of beer, burped and joined in as well. We hadn't told anyone why we were having this little party and so far, nobody asked.

I noticed Cal had gotten pretty chummy with Mr. Jhann`s sister once Mr. Jhann stumbled away in search of a good spot for a nap. I could also see that Bob and Lalia were enjoying each others company and it wasn't long before I saw them heading off on a trail into the tropical foliage.

Kelli and I finally had a chance to be by ourselves and took a swim followed by a long walk down the beach. We picked up sea shells and turned over rocks and watched tiny crabs scurry away. We laughed, kissed, and did everything except talk about the future.

An hour later, as we were strolling back toward our lagoon, Bob and Liala suddenly emerged from the bushes ahead of us, laughing and giggling. When they saw us they stopped suddenly. Bob tried to look serious and said, "Oh, hi you guys. Hey Sonny, do me a favor would you?"

"Sure, what is it?"

"Would you let Cal know that I've decided to resign my position aboard the *Intrepid*?" He paused long enough to look at Liala and then said, "Liala and I have decided to live out the rest of our lives right here on Sleeping Lady!" Bob grabbed Liala around the waist and they both started laughing again.

I winked at Kelli. "Hmm, not a bad idea. You mind if we're your neighbors?"

"Not at all my friend," Bob said over his shoulder as they began to walk away, "you guys can have the other side of the island."

As we watched them walk away I knew it was time to tell Kelli we were leaving. But before I did, I thought a quick dip in the ocean would clear my head, so I waded out in the water then dove in and began swimming like I wasn't coming back. Finally I turned around and swam easily back toward the beach. When the water was waist deep, I stopped and waved to Kelli. "Say, excuse me…Nurse? I'm having a little trouble out here. You think you could help in some way?"

As I watched her wade out to me I marveled again at how lovely she was. When she reached me she slipped her arms around me and laid her head on my shoulder. We stood there a long time, locked together, not saying anything, just letting the gentle waves rock us back and forth. When she finally pushed away from me, I could see tears on her cheeks. "You're leaving, aren't you?"

"Yes," I said.

She looked past my shoulder, out to the ocean, and didn't say anything for a while. Then she said something in Malay that I didn't recognize. But I understood. I pulled her back to me and said, "I love you too."

On the way back from Sleeping Lady island, Kelli was very quiet. I tried to lighten the mood a little by giving the impression that we would be in port for a couple more days. It seemed to be a coward's way out because I knew damn well we'd be leaving the next day, but I just couldn't bring myself to say goodbye.

The thought kept pestering me; *Remember what you're doing here.*

It was just getting dark when we pulled back into the Labuan pier. Most of the guests bowed and thanked us profusely before they disembarked, Mr. Jhann especially. I helped Kelli and Liala off the boat, then kissed Kelli on her cheek. "I'll see you tomorrow, okay?" I said and squeezed her hand.

She smiled sadly. "I've had a wonderful time Sonny."

I wanted to say a hundred things, but a knot in my throat stopped me. I just stood there and watched Kelli and Liala walk down the dock. There was nothing to say.

That night sleep didn't come easy. *How could I be in love with a woman I'd only known for such a short time?* I tried to tell myself that I had become infatuated with Kelli and nothing more. Besides, if she ever found out the real reason I'd come to Labuan, she'd probably hate me.

I tossed and turned and argued with myself until the dream master in my head stepped in to take control. *If you just accept that fact that you love this girl, and you're going to come back to Labuan, I'll let you get some sleep.* I finally gave in and was soon fast asleep.

CHAPTER TWENTY-TWO

Departure

The next morning I got everything in the engine room ready to go while the rest of the crew took on fresh fruits and vegetables and topped off the fresh water tanks. It was an hour before kick-off and I figured I could see Kelli once more to tell her that I wasn't just going to sail out of her life. I wanted her to know that I was coming back. Whatever happened with us then, would happen.

I was just climbing off the boat when a small Asian man wearing a white lab coat and carrying a black satchel, approached me, out of breath. "Sonny Williams?"

"Yeah, that's me."

He had short cropped black hair, dark beady eyes, and when he spoke, saliva formed in the corner of his mouth.

"You must excuse me, but I have to discuss something with you."

"And, you are…?

"I am with the health department. My name is not important."

"Okay, so?"

"I understand you are a…a friend of Miss Kelli's?"

"Yeah. Why? What's goin' on.?"

"We think one of her recently discharged patients may have a strain of typhoid. We are trying to contact anybody even remotely connected with the patient or Miss Kelli."

"Is she okay?" My heart started pounding in my chest.

"Yes, we think she's fine but as I precaution we'd like to inoculate you and your crew."

I gave a sigh of relief. *No biggie*. "Oh, sure, no problem, I said. "In fact I was just on my way to see her."

"I'm afraid I can't allow that Mr. Williams."

My impression of this little turd was getting worse by the second.

"Look, we're leaving in an hour. I just want to tell her something."

"I'm afraid your boat is under official quarantine. The port captain is aware of the situation and until I've administered the crew shots, you won't be allowed to leave. Miss Kelli said to say goodbye."

Now I really didn't like the guy.

I stood there trying to stare him down. Finally, I took a deep breath and said, "Okay, come on."

I took him aboard and explained to the guys what was happening. There was some grumbling but there didn't seem to be an option.

"Let's get the damn shots and get outta here," Cal said.

I got my shot first and went below to start the engines. I was scrambling for last minute options and my right hand shook a little as I set the throttles. *Did I have time to sneak off the boat and run up to Kelli`s or to the hospital?*

After the temperatures and pressures came up on the engine gauges, I climbed up out of the engine room and stepped out on deck. The Asian man had just stepped onto the top rung on the dock ladder.

"You mind throwin' off the lines while you're there?" Cal asked him from outside the wheelhouse.

Shit. We were gone.

"It will be my pleasure," the man said and smiled.

As we eased away from the dock, I saw someone running toward the pier. Kelli! She made it halfway down the dock when suddenly the little bastard reached out and grabbed her. He twisted her by her arm and spun her around.

The moment he touched her, a rage shot through me and I exploded, "God-damn it! Get your FUCKIN' hands off her, you little son-of-a bitch! Don't touch her!" I watched him pull her back the way she'd come. She tried to turn around and I could see her struggling.

"Kelli! Kelli! I'm coming back..." The rumble of the diesels drowned out my words as Cal throttled up and we began separating from the pier. "Please!" I yelled at Kelli. "I'm coming back.... *damn it!* " Rex and Bob came hustling back to see what all the yelling was about. I was shaking.

After I told them what happened, I saw them glance at each other before looking back at me. They didn't say anything but I knew what they were thinking. *Let it go Sonny...Let it go.*

Slowly we made our way up to the wheelhouse and joined Cal. Nobody said anything for a while; we just watched the island grow smaller. Finally, we agreed on a watch schedule and set a course for Viet Nam. Cal stayed at the helm while Bob and Rex headed for the galley. I went below, still shaking.

CHAPTER TWENTY-THREE

South China Sea

On the way to our rendezvous point, we tried to steer clear of any traffic. At night we darkened ship and ran with our running lights off, sometimes slipping between other boats and ships. It was beginning to get a little spooky. At least it kept me from thinking too much about Kelli. My heart ached for her and I planned on calling her as soon as we reached the U.S. In the meantime I knew I had to keep my head out of my ass and I didn't want the rest of the crew to think they couldn't depend on me.

On the third night out, we arrived on station. According to our coordinates we were right where we were supposed to be. A cloud cover hung over us. There was no moon, no stars, and no horizon, just inky blackness. We throttled back to slow ahead and waited for the prescribed time when Cal was supposed to transmit a coded radio message. When the appointed hour arrived, Cal checked our position one more time then began transmitting. His instructions had been to flash our running lights three times on and off while transmitting. If we didn't hear anything, we were to change course forty-five degrees, run for fifteen minutes and repeat.

For hours we transmitted, flashed and changed course. We heard nothing but eerie silence. We saw nothing on the radar. All four of us were on the bridge, waiting, listening. Nothing.

Finally, a static crackle came across the radio: "Motor vessel *Intrepid*...*Intrepid,* please flash your lights...now!"

We answered immediately and did as requested, then waited. And waited. We scanned the radar, but again saw nothing. We strained our eyes looking out into the blackness. Nothing. More time went by. Conversation on the bridge was reduced to hushed tones and whispers. Then suddenly a loud clear voice came over the radio: "*Intrepid*, please put your engines in neutral. We are alongside and will board you port side."

We all jumped. "Holy Shit! I said too loudly. "There he is! Port side!" Like a ghost materializing out of darkness, a fifty-foot wooden fishing boat resembling a Chinese junk slid smoothly along our port rail. Small brown skinned men quickly threw lines around our cleats and made fast to our aft deck. Then a man dressed in a wrap-around sarong and headband jumped aboard. In an Australian accent he said, "Evenin' mates, which one of you be Cal?"

Cal stepped forward. "I'm Cal."

"Well sir, I hope you'll forgive our little cat and mouse routine, but we've been watching you for awhile to make sure you're who you say you are."

"No shit? How`d you get so close without us seeing you?" asked Cal.

The Aussie let out a laugh. "Lets` see, how do you Yanks say it? Tricks of the trade ah `spose`?" His grin grew wider. "Would you like to see what we've brought you?"

"Yes, please," Cal said with a smirk.

The man barked a command to the junk and up popped a small, barefoot, bare-chested man wearing shorts and a black headband. He jumped aboard and set down a black square nylon bundle about three feet long then backed away. The Aussie opened the zippered bag and handed Cal what I assumed to be marijuana sealed in plastic. Cal studied it for a second then held it up to his nose. "No smell. That's good."

"That's right, mate, double wrapped and vacuumed sealed as ordered. And every bale is exactly the same size or nearly so, all in nylon bags, easy to stack. Open it if you'd like."

"Won't be necessary," Cal said as he handed back the package. "We're in business."

The Aussie barked another command and suddenly swarms of worker bees from the boat climbed aboard. We turned our aft deck flood light on and soon bales of pot came flying aboard from the fishing boat. We quickly formed a human chain and started passing bale after bale down to the hold. Bob took charge of directing the workers below and made sure the pot was stacked in the hold as tightly as possible. We really wanted to get all the pot stowed below deck and out of sight. We were prepared to stack bales on the aft deck but that meant securing them and covering everything with tarps. It was hot, sweaty work, but the sense of urgency kept everybody moving at a steady pace.

Finally, after about an hour the bales quit flying up from the Aussie`s boat. I yelled this information down to Bob and told him to take a break. "It's a good thing Sonny," he shouted back up. "We're just about outta` room down here!"

Some of the men sat down, wiped sweat away and drank from something that resembled a boda bag. The Aussie wandered around his crew and conversed with them some kind of dialect before climbing down to his boat. I was getting a little anxious. I was hoping they would get back on their damn boat so we could shut off our lights and get underway.

After a couple of minutes, the Aussie climbed back aboard the *Intrepid* and muttered something to his men. They immediately jumped up and quickly returned to their boat and started to cast off the lines. Then without warning, another boat suddenly appeared out of the blackness and pulled along our starboard side. It was identical in shape and size to the first boat, and before it was even secured alongside, dozens of crew members jumped aboard and bales began to fly again. *What the hell?* Bob hurried to get the tarps ready and started to direct men where to stack bales on the aft deck.

"Okay," Cal blurted to the Aussie. "Just how much pot did you bring?"

Once again, the Aussie apologized for the cat and mouse game, but explained he had taken the precaution of not committing his entire load to us in case we turned out to be 'wrong'. That was the reason they had lingered after they were apparently through loading; they were just giving us a chance to show our true colors once we thought we had all their pot. Once they were satisfied we were okay, the Aussie had radioed his other boats to come alongside.

"Wait a minute` I asked, `Did you say boats`, as in plural?"

"That's right mate, there be three of `em."

After four hours of exhausting non-stop work, we were finally down to the last of the bales. Our hold, where the sleeping quarters had been, was the size of a two-car garage and was completely filled with pot. The aft deck, which was over fifty feet long, was completely covered with bales stacked six feet high. We had bales in the wheelhouse. We had bales in the galley. We had bales forward of the anchor windless. I think we even had a couple of bales in the shower.

Just before the Aussie stepped aboard the last boat to leave, I saw him hand Cal two small objects. Cal examined them for a minute, then looked over at Bob. Cal held the objects up in his hands and asked, "He wants to know if we want to take these with us?"

"What are they?" Bob asked.

"They're hand grenades. In case we want to sink this boat in a hurry."

Bob shrugged and said, "Might as well take `em. I'll put `em in the wheelhouse."

Pot and hand grenades. Nice combo. I went below deck to say a prayer.

CHAPTER TWENTY-FOUR

The next morning, the seas kicked up and soon we were bucking straight into some pretty good-sized waves and swells. As we began taking water over our bow, we noticed some of the unsecured bales we had temporarily stowed forward, were starting to float aft. During the night Rex had done some rough math and figured we had about seventeen tons aboard which made each bale worth about ten thousand dollars. Needless to say, we scrambled to round up the maverick bales. Then after awhile, the seas settled into consistent swells and everything seemed to jiggle itself into place. At last, the compass was pointed towards home.

The next two days were fairly calm and we finally started to relax a little. I started figuring out how soon we would be back to San Francisco. Then I tried to figure out how soon I could get back to Kelli.

I shouldn't have gotten ahead of myself.

The next night, while on watch in the wheelhouse, I noticed a`blip`on the radar screen. It was twenty miles out, headed our way. My pulse kicked up slightly, although I knew it would be silly to think we'd be the only ship out here.

When I checked the radar again I could see our company was still on a reciprocal heading and closing fast. I knew Cal didn't want any of us to change course unless we checked with him first but I thought it wouldn't matter if I tweaked the auto pilot for a few minutes, just enough to put us on a different course than whoever was out there.

I gave it a few minutes then took another look at the screen. I was surprised to find that the other vessel had answered my move with one of his own.

Coincidence? Are we just dancing here?

I immediately turned back to our original compass heading and looked at my watch. I decided to give the contact another five minutes to see what he was going to do. While waiting, I did some rough calculations in my head. *If we're doin` about nine knots, and he's doing the same, and we're about twelve miles apart, we should be seeing each other in about...*

When my brain locked up on the math, I gave up and looked at the screen; the other ship had corrected again, six miles dead ahead.

I hustled below to wake the crew.

It didn't take long for Cal, Bob and Rex to join me in the wheelhouse. Cal took one look at the radar screen then spun around and opened up the locker containing the weapons. He quickly laid the two AR-15`s, the shotgun, and the 45 on the chart table.

This could get ugly.

The contact was now down to five miles on the radar. Nobody said anything. We just stared into the blackness, straining to see with our own eyes what was coming at us. If it's a pirate, we defend ourselves, but what if it's military? We give up and hang?

Is this how it ends for me? No reprieve? It's not like I was on a boat trying to deliver medical supplies to the troops behind enemy lines or running ammunition to the good guys. We're the bad guys! I'm a smuggler for Christ sake!

I guess we were all still hoping that the radar was screwed up. Maybe there's nothing really out there. Maybe we're bouncing our own signal back at us?

Maybe Scotty will beam us up.

Finally, the other ship started to take shape in the darkness. It looked somewhat like a fishing trawler and was a little bigger than the *Intrepid*. We didn't see any markings or insignias. It was heading straight at us.

I glanced at the weapons on the table. They looked cold and sinister and I knew there wasn't one of us aboard that wanted to use them.

We made the decision to maintain our speed and course, and unless the other boat had plans on ramming us, it looked like he could pass, although uncomfortably close, on our port side.

We'd heard nothing on the radio, at least nothing in English we could understand. We were now so close we could see the white water breaking at the ship's bow. As we closed even further, Cal decided we couldn't play this game of chicken any longer and veered to starboard. As we did, we saw the white water on the other boat's bow diminish and its running lights swing, indicating it had slowed and had turned to face us at a ninety-degree angle. Moments later, as we passed within fifty yards of his bow, a powerful search light illuminated from the boat and began raking us from bow to stern. Then the light seemed to linger on our flag above the wheelhouse.

As our stern passed the other boat's bow we could see black smoke pour out of the exhaust stacks as the vessel turned to follow us. There was a deck light on and we could see several scraggly looking guys uncovering the tarps on a small speedboat that was on the aft deck. A couple of them had machetes on their hips. My heart was really pounding now as the boat slipped in behind us.

"What the hell is this guy up to?" Cal screamed. "What the fuck`s he want?"

Then the radio crackled and a voice with a foreign accent pierced the air. "Ello `Merikan ship. `Merika ship please."

Cal hesitated then grabbed the mike. "Go ahead."

"You stop now. You stop now, yes?"

"Why? Who are you?!"

"Ahh,...navy...we navy. You stop now."

Cal turned to us and asked, "You guys see a flag?"

We all shook our heads no.

"We don't see a flag. What country are you?" Cal said into the mike, buying some time.

"We navy. You stop!"

"Sure," Cal said to himself more than anybody else. Then he looked at us and said, "These guys ain't navy, you know that don't you?" Without waiting for an answer, he put his hand on the throttles.

"Sure asshole... sure we're gonna stop!" Cal said as he advanced the throttles to their limits. It was our turn to pour black smoke.

Unfortunately all it did was signal our intention. As low as we were in the water, the extra power didn't help much. We weren't going to outrun this guy.

Within minutes he was about a hundred yards off our port side. The radio cracked again, "`Merikan boat ...stop! Stop now, we have guns, we shoot!"

The boat was slowly closing the distance between us as a couple of deckhands moved up to the bow. One man hoisted something onto his shoulders, something that looked like....

Holy shit, a rocket launcher! Jesus Christ! Is this really happening?

"`Merikan boat, you stop. Now!"

Rex started to say something when we saw a flash from their bow and a missile whistled into the sea directly in front of us.

"Jesus Christ, whadda we do?" Bob yelled. "They'll stop us sure as shit if they hit us with one of those!"

"Hold your fire!" Cal screamed into the mike.

"Okay, all right, we gotta do something here you guys," Rex said. I noticed he was shaking. "What?" He asked, his voice raising an octave. "Just what the hell do we do here?'...Come on, whadda we do??!!"

It seemed like a dream, but above the pounding of my heart I heard myself say, "Let's give `em the boat."

Bob immediately jumped in, "We can't just give up, they'll kill us!"

I knew the inflatable was hooked up to the starboard davit, the outboard motor still connected to five gallons of gas. "Okay, look," I said, "the Zodiac's on our starboard side, they can't see it. If Cal can stall `em long enough we can get the Zodiac ready so we can get outta here in that. We'll have to come to an almost dead stop but if we keep our boat in the same position to theirs, we can launch the Zodiac, slip over the side and disappear in the dark before they see what we're doing. We'd probably be too small to find us on their radar, besides, they don't care about us, they just want the boat."

"I'm not going to give `em this boat," Cal said through clenched teeth.

"Okay Skip, listen," I said. "I can open up the sea chest in the engine room and start flooding her right now. And I'll open up the engine room portholes so when we push off in the Zodiac, we can toss in those grenades to make sure she sinks."

Cal stared at me for several moments without saying anything. Finally he raised the mike, "Hold your fire, we're slowing now." Then to us, "Okay, Rex, you and Bob get the Zodiac ready. Sonny, do your thing in the engine room. Get back here as soon as you can."

Bob and Rex scrambled out the starboard side of the wheel-house and down to the Zodiac. I made it to the engine room as fast as I could and opened the sea chest and began flooding the *Intrepid.*

Bob and Rex had the small inflatable ready to launch in less than two minutes. We all hurried back and joined Cal on the bridge. He was at the wheel with the two grenades and an M-15 lying on the console next to him. I was shocked to see how close the other boat was to us now. We didn't have much time.

"We're ready Cal. Put her in neutral, let's go!" Bob said.

Then a blinding searchlight lit up our wheelhouse and a voice boomed over the radio: "You raise hands! All you…step outside. Raise hands now!"

We all froze for a moment. And then Cal snapped. Moving with surprising speed, he slammed the throttles forward and spun the wheel towards the blinding light. As the *Intrepid* heeled over, Cal grabbed an M-15, stepped outside and started blasting away.

"You want my boat?!" he screamed. "You want my boat, motherfuckers!!?? Okay, here's my fuckin` boat right up your goddamn ass!!"

The searchlight went out as Cal emptied a clip at the oncoming boat. The rest of us ducked down, hugging the deck as Cal kept screaming and shooting. Then I noticed the wheel spinning out of control. On the edge of panic, I crawled over to it and held on for dear life. Bullets started thudding into the side of our boat and breaking out glass on the bridge.

Rex stuck his head up and looked out. "Oh no, oh Jesus we're gonna hit..."

Bam! The sound of scraping and crunching followed the jarring as the two boats collided at a forty-five degree angle. Our port side life raft and a gas and oil drum broke loose from our upper boat deck and crashed down on the other boat. Our bow rode up their starboard side and stayed pinned there. Cal jumped back inside, grabbed the hand grenades and frantically tried to pull the pin on one of them. In desperation he threw one down at the boat. Nothing. He went to throw the other one when Bob stopped him.

"Cal, squeeze the handle first! You gotta squeeze…here, give it to me!" Bob grabbed it out of Cal's hand, pulled the pin and threw it. It bounced off the deck started rolling aft, and then exploded.

"Let's get outta here!" Bob yelled. We started out of the wheelhouse when suddenly a second and bigger explosion rocked us. The gasoline drum that had landed on the pirates` boat during the collision had exploded, knocking our bow back off the other ship. As the two boats began to break away, Cal jumped back to the helm, grabbed the wheel and put it hard over before shoving the throttles forward again.

Bits of fire and debris fluttered down on the *Intrepid* as she sluggishly responded to Cal`s commands. Time stood still as we slowly began to separate from the other boat which now had flames licking up towards it's wheelhouse. Small patches of fire clung to our port bow as we gained even more separation.

"Go baby, go!!" Cal pleaded to *his* boat.

Oh shit, the engine room! Quickly I ran down the ladder. Dirty, oily water was already lapping above the deck plates. Frantically I felt for the sea chest and secured it. I flipped on the bilge pump and prayed that it wouldn't short out. Meanwhile Rex and Bob hustled to extinguish the fires along our port side.

As I ran up out of the engine room I noticed we were still putting distance between us and the other boat. When I rejoined Cal, he had his hand on the throttles and was urging the *Intrepid* on. "Come on sweetheart... come on baby...that's it, that's it.... you can do it. Go!"

Rex and Bob scrambled up the outside ladder and rushed into the wheelhouse.

"Everybody okay?" Bob asked. "Cal? You all right?"

"Come on baby, come on...Yeah, I'm good."

I noticed how badly Cal was shaking. Hell, we were all shaking.

"Damn, we took quite a shot there when we collided but I don't see a hole or anything," Rex said excitedly. "I think we're still sea worthy. Hot damn!"

We all just stood there, trying to catch our breath...letting our hearts slow down.

The flames from the other boat continued to dance in the night, but they seemed to be getting smaller and farther away.

We stood in the wheelhouse and shook.

Twenty minutes later we were still shaking, but the flames from the other boat were just small flickers behind us. Then nothing.

Finally we were alone in the dark.

CHAPTER TWENTY-FIVE

The next few days we spent licking our wounds, literally and figuratively. Cal made an awkward attempt to explain his actions and offered a half-assed apology. "I've made this trip before, but never as a captain. And to be honest with you, I…I really don't have much experience handling a boat."

We thanked him for saving our lives and told him to shut up.

Rex discovered a splintered boat railing hanging off our bow anchor and saved it as a souvenir. Bob wondered how much the old man was going to deduct from our wages for the new gouges and dents in the boat. I cleaned the engine room and wondered if I was going to make it home alive.

We all could feel a new level of unspoken respect for each other and I think silently we also thanked our individual Gods. Little by little we settled back into the routine of running the boat. Sailing on to the blissful hum of the diesels I let my heart slow down to match the unsuspecting engines` steady rhythm.

I thought of Kelli and smiled.

For the next ten days we enjoyed good weather and calm seas. What ships we saw during the day passed us by without interest. The little blips on the radar at night went about their own business. We sailed through the South China Sea and around the northern tip of the Philippines without further incident. It wasn't until we were well into the Pacific Ocean that we encountered the storm.

We first noticed the weather patterns were changing on our weather fax. Then we started picking up radio reports that some heavy stuff was headed our way. After awhile the seas began building in an ominous way. Then before we knew it, the winds picked up and we started getting kicked around pretty good. More and more we tried to quarter into the growing waves, some of them breaking ten feet above us. The wind picked up even more and began making a whistling, screaming sound. Then, in a violent lurch, the load on the aft deck shifted, putting us in a dangerous port list. The wind continued to hammer us from starboard and the situation was deteriorating quickly. I knew we had to ballast seawater to starboard as soon as possible.

But before we could do anything, we had to address another problem: the load on the aft deck. We'd have to block or brace the load against the starboard rail before we began ballasting so it wouldn't shift back and throw us into a starboard list.

Tearing apart wooden pallets that held our life rafts, Bob and Rex quickly braced the load as best they could. I started the ballast pump and prayed.

At first it was hard to tell if we were doing any good. The prospect of trying to level anything in these seas seemed almost silly. But slowly, and surely, the Intrepid began to right herself.

As the storm raged on, it was impossible to do anything but hang on. Nobody could eat or drink anything. Sleep was out of the question. The best place to be was on the bridge in the captain's chair. You could loop your arms through the armrests and brace your legs against the console. But the captain's chair also meant you had a clear view of what the ocean was throwing our way. We were riding a roller coaster of monster waves, each one larger than the last. With each wave I'd think, "Oh Christ, this is it!" Then somehow we'd ride the wave straight up, heel nauseatingly to one side, then plummet straight down to the bottom of the next trough. The mirrors we had aboard shattered from concussions. Nobody could clean up the glass; it was too dangerous to try. If you had to piss, you pretty much did it where you stood.

Or at least you tried. This went on for two days. Then things got worse.

As difficult as it was, it was still necessary to go through the engine room every hour or so to check on things. It was during one of these trips that I heard the piercing squeal of an alarm. It was the low-level water alarm for the port engine cooling system. A quick check showed that the sight glass on the water expansion tank was empty and the temperatures on the gauges were climbing into the red. I quickly filled the expansion tank, which quieted the alarm. Soon the temperatures began to return to normal. Hoping against hope that I had solved the problem, I made my way back up to the wheelhouse to monitor the gauges from there. Two hours later, the temperatures on the port engine began inching up again.

This time I stayed in the engine room after refilling the tank. Without sounding the fresh water tank I couldn't be sure how much water we had left, but I knew we couldn't just keep refilling the port engine. Thirty minutes later, the alarm sounded again.

Now back in the wheelhouse I explained the situation to Cal. We were going to have to secure the port engine long enough for me to troubleshoot it. The danger was, we were barely making headway into the wind now, and with only one engine, we'd hardly be making any headway at all. Cal would have to do everything he could with the starboard engine to keep us squared into the waves. If we got sideways in the seas, we could capsize. With no other choice, I headed back down to the engine room.

With Bob's help, I began pulling one of the water pumps off the front of the engine. I was hoping that maybe one of the thermostat valves had stuck and we'd be able to replace or repair it fairly quickly. Looking back, I should have known that wasn't the answer, but in my sleep-deprived mind, it was the only thing I could think of at the time. It was an extremely difficult task. Everything on the engine was scorching hot. We tried placing watered down rags where we could to keep from burning our hands, but invariably the boat would lurch, toss us off balance, and we'd grab the wrong thing. When we finally got the pump off I was able to inspect the valves; they were fine. Hurriedly we put the pump back together, filled up the tank, and got the engine running again. I knew this was only buying us another forty-five minutes before we'd have to shut it down again, but I was hoping I could think of something else to do in the meantime. Somehow we *had* to keep this engine running. Then through the foggy caverns of my pea-brain, a thought occurred to me: we didn't have much fresh water left but we *did* have an endless supply of salt water! If I could somehow jury-rig the ballast pump to suck seawater to the engine, we could cool the engine with salt water! It would mean we'd trash the engine sooner or later, but dammit, we needed that engine back on line now! We feverishly began some makeshift plumbing.

I cannibalized parts from where I could, including some plumbing from our toilet. After about an hour and a half I had something that looked like a bootlegger's still attached to the front of the engine. As soon as I made the last of the connections, I stopped and stared at Bob. For a second we just stood there and looked at each other. Bob shrugged and gave a me a, "what-the-hell-let`s-try-it look." I started the ballast pump, and lit off the engine.

With salt water circulating through the system, I shifted the engine back in gear. The needle on the temperature gauge immediately shot up into the red for a heartbeat or two but then settled back down.

An hour later, the temperatures were still holding and we were indicating a forward speed of three knots.

The storm seemed to rage on forever, but everything held together. Finally, out of pure exhaustion, I lay down on a cradle of pot, and mercifully fell asleep.

CHAPTER TWENTY-SIX

The next morning I awoke to an odd humming sound. Too tired to get up and still half asleep, I lay there, eyes closed, and tried to identify the vaguely familiar sound. It sounded like…a refrigerator. Yeah, that's what it is. Then the sound clicked off. A refrigerator? My eyes flew open. It *was* a refrigerator! I was hearing the refrigerator in the galley! The wind was quiet. The storm was over!!

I climbed the ladder and joined Bob in the wheelhouse. Above the horizon the sun was peeking out between scattered clouds. The ocean was dirty and foamy looking, but the swells were far apart and rolling gently. I looked at the ship's clock, "Goddamn, what time is it? I've slept through my watch!"

"Not to worry my friend," Bob said. "The way you were out, well, I just didn't have the heart to wake you."

"Well then," I offered, "I'll just have to buy you a few hundred beers when we get to Mexico."

"It's a deal," Bob said with a wink.

The next few days we spent tending our wounds again and putting the boat back together. Both main engines were purring along just fine, so I let `em continue to do just that. After a few more days of enjoyable, monotonous cruising, Cal announced, "I've made radio contact with our off-load people. We'll meet up tomorrow."

I smiled as I thought of how Tim and I would be celebrating soon. I thought how sweet it was going to be to get back to Kelli. I thought about how I was never going to set foot on another boat again.

I also had to remind myself that this little adventure was not over yet.

The next day when we reached our co-ordinates, we had no problem raising our contact on the radio. Nor did they just suddenly appear of the night. In fact, it was a bright sunny morning when a sixty-foot fishing trawler motored right up to us and secured to our starboard side. And, instead of swarms of Thai sailors, there were only five English-speaking guys whom I assumed were Americans.

They greeted us with pleasantries, fresh fruits, a case of cold beer, and a Playboy magazine. Cal said, "Yeah, great to see you too. Now where you gonna put all this shit?"

"Well, *we* can't take your whole load, but we'll take what you've got there on deck. There'll be another boat meeting you tomorrow morning."

We began tossing bales of pot like men possessed.

Delighted to have the deck cleared of pot, we fired up our main engines and continued on course, getting ever close to home and the end of our odyssey. Just one more stop to off-load the stash in our hold and we were home free. We toasted each other with our present of beer and threw fresh fruit at each other. We ogled Miss May and slapped each other on the back. We were a happy crew.

Then the plane flew over.

"What's a matter Sonny?" asked Rex, "It was just a plane."

"No, it wasn't *just* a plane," I said. "It was a frickin` navy P-3. A patrol plane!"

"So? We're only three days out of San Francisco. It's probably on a routine patrol."

Yeah, maybe. But I didn't like the way the plane flew low over us twice before disappearing over the horizon. My worries grew later that evening when we picked up something on the radar that was circling us and moving way too fast to be a boat. It had to be the plane. Annoyingly, the blip on the screen blinked constantly. Then we picked up another contact twelve miles directly behind us.

"I gotta tell you guys," I began, "I think somethin`s up. We've had steady company above and behind us for the last three hours."

"Well, don't forget Sonny," Cal said. "We *are* close to the mainland and the San Francisco shipping lanes. We should expect traffic."

"Yeah, but why is the guy behind us all of a sudden doing the same speed we are? And the plane continuing to circle? What's up with that?"

"Well, we don't know for sure if that blip on the screen is a plane do we?" asked Rex.

"We haven't really seen anything with our own eyes. And the guy behind us could be our off-load guy, or he could be just headed to San Francisco. Besides, there's not a lot we can do about it now anyway, is there?"

"Well, we *could* toss the rest of the load overboard," I suggested. We'd have to slice open each bale so they'd sink so the guy behind us wouldn't see any of it. It'd probably take us five hours to toss it all, but we could be done by sunrise."

I took a deep breath. *My god, I'm talking like a long time smuggler now.*

We stood there in silence, each of us weighing the options. Then Cal pretty much answered the question by asking one of his own: "Okay, Sonny, let's say we do what you suggest and it turns out you're wrong. You wanna` be the one to tell the old man that three days out of San Francisco, we threw away twenty million dollars of his load?"

He had a point. We decided to wait and see what the morning would bring.

I didn't get any sleep that night worrying about the situation we were in. *If you can't do the time, don't do the crime.* I thought about Tim and the possible consequences of what may lie ahead. Remembering what Tim had said about the old man putting up money to bail us out didn't help much either.

At three in the morning, I climbed up to the bridge and relieved Rex on watch. The first thing I did was look at the radar screen. Our company was still in their relative positions. We had two and a half hours until sunrise.

As a gray light filtered into the morning, I looked at the radar and saw that the ship behind us had picked up speed. I knew I'd be able to see it with glasses at any minute. Part of me wanted to pick up the binoculars, and part of me didn't. I gave it another five minutes before I picked them up.

My heart sank. The orange stripe showed clearly against the white bow. *United States Coast Guard.*

Stunned, I set the glasses down and took a deep breath. Maybe he'll just take a cursory look at us and continue on his way. Maybe he's not interested in us at all. Then the four-engine turbo prop plane, with its orange stripes across the wings, appeared low on the horizon and made a pass directly over us.

Once again I had to wake the crew with the likelihood of bad news. Five minutes later the radio confirmed my fears. "This is the United States Coast Guard, put your engines in neutral, gather all hands on the fantail, and stand by to be boarded."

CHAPTER TWENTY-SEVEN

The Coast Guard boarded the *Intrepid* with weapons drawn. A blond, fresh-faced lieutenant in full battle gear ordered us to sit down on the deck and place our hands on our heads, then he gave the command to two enlisted men to conduct a quick search below deck.

They weren't gone long. When they returned, they nodded to the lieutenant, who then turned to us with a smirk. "*You have the right to remain silent. Anything you say, can, and will be used against you...*"

I was almost nauseous as I felt the handcuffs clicked tightly in place behind my back. After all that we'd been through, it came down to this. I knew all along that getting arrested was a possibility, but I couldn't believe it was really happening.

Look, we're not the bad guys! We aren't a threat to national security or anything. We're all Americans here. I'm a U.S. Navy veteran, for Christ's sake!

We were transferred to the Coast Guard cutter and were surprised to find they didn't have a place to put us. We spent the first night aboard the cutter in leg irons and handcuffed to posts and chairs while they put together a makeshift brig.

I desperately wanted to get word to Tim about our situation and asked one of the sailors standing guard if I could make my allotted phone call. He laughed, and looked at me like I was an idiot. "We're at sea, man. We ain't got no telephones!" But he must have mentioned my request to someone with a brain because it wasn't long before the captain showed up in person and denied my request. Something about national security.

Five days after being arrested on the high seas, the Coast Guard ingloriously towed the *Intrepid* back under the Golden Gate bridge to Treasure Island. Television crews and cameras met us as we were transferred off the cutter to cars waiting to take us downtown. We were a spectacle. The headline of the week apparently. For the first time in my life, I realized people were looking at me for what I was; a criminal. Now all I could hope for, or any of us for that matter, was whoever this old man was, he'd be good for his word and bail us out as soon as possible.

As we were being booked into the San Francisco jail, I noticed a television set on the wall. There was a newscast showing an earlier aerial view of our arrest at sea as well as our arrival in port. I was shocked to see how damaged and beat up the *Intrepid* looked; it hardly appeared seaworthy. We didn't look much better as the camera panned to the four of us, scruffy and solemn, being led down a gang plank in leg irons and handcuffs.

We were stripped-searched and given blue jumpsuits along with a bedroll and a towel. Then we were taken to a large cell with twenty-five bunk beds. Problem was, there were already sixty prisoners in the cell.

"Inside," the jailer said, prodding us unceremoniously into the lion's den.

A couple of guys were lying on their bunks and laughed while we stood there trying to figure out what to do next. Finally, an extremely thin man with no discernible teeth said, "Hey, you can bunk with sweet thing. He's three bunks down on your right. He likes company." The local meth-head jerked his head and yelled over his shoulder, "Don't you sweet thing?"

"Oh fuck you!" came an answer.

"You wish!"

As we made our way down to the end of the cell I tried not to make eye contact with anybody. I found a small space on the floor in a corner and opened my bedroll. The rest of the crew found places on the other side of the cell.

A black guy with a split lip and a badly broken nose came up to me."Hey man, what's yo beef"?

"I ain't got no problem," I said, with a sigh. "Is this your spot?"

"No man, I mean, whaddya down for? Whacha guys do to get here?"

"We had some pot," I said, still trying to act like being in jail was no big deal for me.

"Dat's cool. Bring any witcha?" He laughed.

"Not this time."

"How much dey nail you wid?"

"Not sure how much we had aboard, probably a few__"

"Aboard? Hey, you da dudes on tee-vee? Wid da boat?"

"Yeah, I guess so."

"Hey dig this," he said, turning to a couple of guys. "Deese the guys on dat boat! `Member? The one's we saw on da tube with all dat pot!"

"No shit"? The tallest white guy I'd ever seen, balding, and covered in tattoos, got up from a bunk and came over to join us. "That's what I got popped for too man. `Course I didn't have as much you," he cackled. Then he turned serious. "I guess you'll be outta here pretty soon, huh?"

"I dunno, maybe."

"Yeah, you big guys got all them fancy lawyers and shit. Betcha` you're outta here in no time."

"Yeah, well...maybe. We'll see. Right now I just wanna lie down for a while. Haven't had much sleep lately. You know how it is."

"Yeah, cool. Hey, my name's Lester. You need anything, let me know. I'll talk with you later, man."

That night was one of the longest of my life. I was allowed to make my phone call but couldn't get a hold of Tim. I kept imagining all the worst-case scenarios, but figured things would look better in the morning. I stuck wadded up toilet paper in my ears to try and drown out all the noise and jive that resonated throughout the cell even after the lights went out. I tossed and turned on the three-inch mattress that separated me from the concrete floor.

Finally, around two a.m., I nodded off. I dreamed I was in jail.

"Count time! Count time! Everybody up!" Six a.m. and all sixty-four of us in the cell had twenty minutes to use the three toilets and get back to our bunks for headcount.

Somehow that got accomplished and then we all lined up single file and passed by the cell door. Something resembling scrambled eggs, black coffee and toast on a steel tray was passed through a slot in the door.

Cal, Bob, Rex and I found a place to sit down at the metal table in the middle of the cell.

We kept our voices low and talked about our situation. We reminded each other not to say too much to anybody until we heard from a lawyer.

"It'll probably be Monday before we hear from someone," Cal said. "We'll just have to cool it till then."

"Let me know if you don't want those eggs," said a large shadow looming behind me. I turned. Lester. He broke into a grin.

"Ya gotta get used to `em." He squeezed in beside me.

I took one bite of the watered down whatever they were and gave the rest to him.

"Think you'll get out today?" he asked, shoveling the slop into his mouth.

We all shrugged.

"Oh, yeah, you guys are *feds*. They'll probably move you come Monday. They'll dress you up in those federal orange suits, `stead of these city blues. I bet you get out then, huh?"

"Maybe," snorted Cal, "maybe not."

"Yeah, federal prisoners got it made. I hear there are only twelve guys to a cell. Better food too".

Not wanting to carry the conversation further, we all eased away from the table and took our trays back to the slot in the cell door. Then without anything else to do, we headed back to our respective places on the concrete slab.

Saturday slipped into Sunday afternoon without a word from anybody. Then Sunday's evening newscast grabbed our attention: "Recapping this week's news, we've just learned that the boat intercepted by the coast guard last week carried over seventeen tons of high grade marijuana from Thailand. It has been valued at approximately fifty million dollars. Channel Five's news team asked coast guard commander, Captain Tom Daily if this could just be the tip of the iceberg as far as smuggling operations go."

"Hey! You guys are on TV again!" someone yelled. "Fifty million! God damn, dudes, you sure fucked up!"

Heads around the TV looked back at us for a reaction. All we could do was nod and agree with them. Then under his breath Rex said, "Well, somebody fucked up, that's for sure."

Later that night Lester asked if one of us wanted his bunk. He said he didn't mind sleeping on the floor. "Just remember me, man. You know, in case your friends wanna bail me out too. I'm a good wheel man."

CHAPTER TWENTY-EIGHT

On Monday morning the four of us were transferred to the federal section of the jail where we were split up. Bob and Rex shared a cell across from mine but I had no idea where Cal ended up. Lester was right about the fed cells being smaller, only holding twelve prisoners to a cell. Lester had failed to mention, however, the different caliber of the clientele. Six of the prisoners in my cell were awaiting murder charges.

Later that day, I was finally able to reach Tim by phone. This time I wasn't the bearer of bad news. He'd already heard all about it, along with the rest of the West Coast.

"You all right"? he asked.

"Yeah, I guess so."

"Goddamn, I'm sorry I got you into this."

"Me too, I sighed. "But nobody held a gun to my head."

"Yeah, but still, if I hadn't been such a fuck-up you wouldn't be there now."

I couldn't argue with him. "Well, let's just hope I can get outta here soon. I haven't heard from anybody. You know anything? What's up with the old man? I'm beginning to feel like we're gonna get screwed."

"I'll make some calls…see what's goin` on."

"Thanks."

"How'd you get caught?"

"I dunno, nobody's said yet."

"Okay, maybe I can find something out about that too."

"Be careful."

"Will do. Ah….Sonny?"

"Yeah?"

"Hang in there man, I'll get you outta there."

"Please do."

The next day we were taken out of our cells for our arraignment. I was shocked at the number of charges. The prosecutor kept rattling off so many different indictment counts that I wasn't sure exactly what I'd even done. Finally he said the one I could understand: conspiracy to import marijuana. Bail was set at one hundred thousand dollars.

The next day I was led to a small room with two chairs, a table and a man I assumed was my new attorney, the one the old man had finally sent.

I quickly realized that it's very disconcerting to meet a well-dressed lawyer when you're in orange jump suit. The man introduced himself as Dean L. Tishure, Attorney at Law.

Well, la-di-fucking-da.

Mr. Tishure`s hair was combed back in the perfect pompadour with just a hint of silver in all the right places. His cologne was almost as nauseating as his smile. After I shook his hand, we both awkwardly tried to offer each other a chair. Neither one of us seemed sure of who the guest was here.

He began by offering his references and experiences in these types of cases. I let him rattle on for a while, then fearful our time would run out, I interrupted him and asked about the charges against me. As he explained the counts he also mentioned the maximum prison time associated with each one. When he finally finished I did a quick tally in my mind. *Ninety-seven years!*

"Now keep in mind those are maximum times and you'd have to be found guilty on each count. I'm just giving you a worst case scenario. But I can tell you right now they'll probably drop at least half of those as we get closer to sentencing."

"Oh thank god, what a relief," I said. "That'd only be forty-eight and a half years!"

He scowled. Mr. Attorney at Law was obviously not a fan of client flippancy.

"Now obviously, they'll want to deal," the lawyer began. "And as I understand it, your degree of culpability is much less than, say, the captain's, right? Or whomever is behind this operation? Now this is entirely up to you of course, but if there are names that you'd be willing to give the prosecution, that would reduce… well, you probably know how that game works."

I was shocked. "Well, you sure as hell don't want me to do that now do you? The old man would have me killed."

"I'm not sure I follow you."

"Didn't the old man send you here?"

"You…you mean your father?"

"My father? No, I mean…wait a minute, what`re you doing here? Who are you?"

"As I told you, I'm an experienced attorney in these type of cases. I saw your arrest on television and as it happens, I have a break in my workload. That's why I asked if you'd like to meet with me. I'm here to offer you my services."

"You came on your own? Nobody sent you?"

"That's correct."

"And you're offering your services…for a fee?"

"Well, yes of course, but I can assure you that I will work diligently on your behalf. You may even be aware of some of the cases I've been involved in. For instance, there was__"

"How much?"

"Fifty thousand," he said. "That includes going to trial if it comes to that."

He must have noticed the air going out of my balloon.

"It seems you were expecting someone else? I mean you *are* entitled to a public defender, and most of them do a fine job, but, well, you know, they also have quite a workload. I guess it comes down to that old saying, `you get what you pay for`."

As I was led back to my cell I wondered how I could pay for anything.

The next couple of days were more of the same. I met with at least half a dozen attorneys offering their services. None of them knew anything about the old man.

I had been in jail ten days when Tim showed up in the regular visitors` room. Unlike the room I had been allowed to meet in privately with lawyers, this one had a glass partition and telephone hook ups. There were six or seven other prisoners and visitors on either side of me.

I hadn't actually seen Tim since I'd sailed off on this adventure almost three months ago. He looked drawn and tense, and said he had good news, bad news.

"I've asked Jamie to get a hold of the old man but so far no luck. It's like suddenly nobody knows shit about anything. I don't like what's goin` on here, you should've heard from someone by now. I'm not going to let you sit in here and rot. So here's what I'm thinking. If we combine our cash, we've got around fifteen thousand…right?" I gave a weak nod. "Okay, well, I found a bondsman who says he'll take the equity in Mom's house as collateral for the rest of your bail. It'll take a couple of days to work out the paperwork but I think you could be outta here by the end of the week. Whadda you think?"

"I think hell yes, do it," I said. "I can't breathe in here!"

"Okay, I'll get the ball rollin`. You just hang in there. Meantime I'll try and find some answers." He left me with his best Dezi Arnez imitation: "Someone has some `splainin` to do!"

CHAPTER TWENTY-NINE

Although I didn't like the news about the old man, or lack thereof, I was encouraged by Tim's visit. Even though it had taken ten days to come up with a plan, if he could put something together to get me out, I'd be able to breathe fresh air, and clear my head enough to think straight. In the meantime a parade of attorneys continued to come. Apparently lawyers not only chase ambulances, they watch the news too. Unfortunately, none of them were there courtesy of the old man.

I had noticed that with each attorney's subsequent visit, the price tag on their fees seemed to be going down. Even their demeanor and dress were somewhat less than Dean L. Tishure had shown. I guess we were becoming old news.

The lawyer that came calling the day after Tim's visit was older and needed a haircut and a shoeshine. For lack of anything better to do, I pretty much told him my whole story while he sat there and listened patiently. I guess I needed to get everything off my chest. When I finished he just sat there nodding like he was mulling something over. Finally he cleared his throat and began to speak. He didn't talk nearly as quickly or as eloquently as the others, but he had news that sent my head spinning and rocked my heart.

"Well son, I assume someone has explained to you by now about your 'Right of Discovery`?"

It was my turn to nod and he went on.

"Well then you know you have the right to know just exactly how you got caught, right?"

Again I nodded but began to feel that maybe this old guy had something the others didn't.

"Well, I've found out through a source of mine in the Justice Department that the prosecution doesn't want to disclose this right of discovery to you. They'd just as soon not tell you right now how you got caught. Now, from where I sit, I figure this means a couple of things. Number one, they don't want to give you this information just yet because they want to catch more smugglers in the same manner that they caught you, and number two, and most importantly to you, if you do decide to give up your right of discovery it may mean you can use that as a bargaining chip for a reduced sentence. We could probably get it down to seven years. With time off for good behavior, you might be lookin` at five or less. Now, from what you've just told me, I take it you don't really care how you guys were caught, do you?"

"No, not really." I started to breathe a little easier and even added with a laugh, "I'm curious, but as I told you, I don't have any intention of continuing in this career." The thought of five years in prison was still hard to digest but it was certainly a lot more manageable than Tishure`s guess of a few years short of a century.

"Well, I've given you enough to chew on for now. If you decide you'd like my services, here's my card."

As he started to leave I couldn't help ask, "So, did your friend in the Justice Department tell you how we got caught, or is that an unethical question?"

"The question itself is not unethical but the way I found out sure as hell is. And if you even mention it to anybody, you could ruin a couple of careers and mess up this whole deal. It won't bother me much `cause I'm about ready to retire, but it could screw you up bad if the wrong people know you found out how you were popped."

For some reason it suddenly became terribly important to know why I was sitting here in jail. I knew I wouldn't say anything given what was at stake.

He had one hand on the doorknob when I asked, "Okay, how'd we get caught?"

He looked straight at me and said, "Well, I don't know what the probable cause might be just yet but I *do* know you were set up. Someone planted a tracking device on your boat while you were on the island of Labuan. The feds had you the whole way. My source didn't tell me exactly who it was that planted the device, but he did tell me it was put there by a nurse.

The door clicked shut behind him.

The shock stayed with me through the night. I was devastated. If it *was* Kelli that planted the transmitter, who was she working for? Was she a D.E.A agent? Had I been that badly fooled? I tried to imagine that maybe the old lawyer had some bum information.

As the night wore on I began to understand the expression, *hardened criminal.* It wasn't that the criminal got physically stronger or tougher, it was the heart that hardened.

I was still struggling with my thoughts the next morning when the jailer appeared at my cell door, rattling his keys. "Williams! Get up. You've made bail."

CHAPTER THIRTY

I still had all my emotional baggage but at least I was standing outside in fresh air. I was greatly relieved to be out of jail, but disappointed that Tim wasn't there. I opened the envelope the bondsman had left for me. Inside was an airplane ticket, a hundred dollars in cash, and a note from Tim. "I think Jamie's got some info on the old man. I'll see you at the house. T."

An hour later I was at the San Francisco airport.

On the flight home to Seattle I had time to reflect on how much my life had changed in the last few months. The words from a Shakespeare play kept rolling through my head: "*Things without all remedy, should be without regard, what's done is done.*"

If only it were that simple.

The house was dark when the taxi pulled up to the curb. It was late and I was tired but it was good to be home and it was going to be good to be with my brother again. The only problem was Tim wasn't there. Or at least his truck wasn't. As I walked past the driveway, I could see that he had been there recently from the small drips of oil reflecting in the streetlight. Tim's truck always left a unique pattern of oil that reminded me of the Big Dipper in the night sky, or as he called it, "the Big *Dripper*."

I looked around the house for a note or something, but found nothing. Not even a beer in the fridge. I thought about calling Jamie but decided I should probably talk with Tim first. I sat on the couch and watched some late night television I tried to stay awake, but my eyelids were way too heavy to cooperate.

It was eight in the morning when I opened my eyes. It took me a second or two to realize I wasn't in jail anymore.

After a trip to the bathroom, I looked around the kitchen for something to eat but the only thing I could find was a package of frost-covered waffles in the freezer. I did find some coffee so I put that on. Then I called Jamie.

"Hello."

His voice stunned me and for a moment I couldn't say anything. I thought about if Jamie hadn't of done what he did, we wouldn't be in this mess.

"Hello?" he said again.

"Ah, Jamie?"

"Yeah?"

"It's Sonny."

"Sonny?! Oh shit. Are you okay? Hey listen, I'm real sorry…"

He was stumbling all over himself until I cut him off. "Jamie, I was supposed to meet Tim at our mother's house, but he's not here. You know where he is?"

"No, no I don't. What are you---?"

"When was the last time you talked with him?"

"Let's see, ah, yesterday I guess. Yeah, yesterday morning. He's been trying to get a hold of, well, you know who."

"Yeah I know. What`d you tell him. What`d you tell Tim?"

"Ah, I'm a little uncomfortable talking about this over the phone…."

"Jamie, right now I don't give a shit whether you're comfortable or not. I'm trying to find my brother. Now what did you tell him?"

"All I said was that I didn't know how to get a hold of the old man. He always got a hold of me if he needed to. I haven't talked to the old man since you left."

"That's it? That was the whole conservation?"

"Yeah, pretty much....oh, I mentioned I did see the old man a couple of times up in the Magnolia Bluff area. He was driving a brown Chevy pickup. It had some lettering on the side, like a construction company or something."

"Well thanks for nothing Jamie," I said bitterly. "I'll talk to you later."

"Look, Tim`ll show up soon. I'm sorry about everything..."

"Save it Jamie. Let me know if you hear from Tim."

I hung up and went back to the kitchen and poured myself a cup of coffee. There didn't seem to be anything I could do but to sit tight until I heard from Tim.

As I waited I decided to tell Tim to forget about trying to get the old man to help us. It didn't matter anymore. I wanted to wash my hands of all the bad shit. I didn't want Tim involved with these guys at all. I was sure I could work something out with the lawyer who was about to retire, and if not, there was always a public defender. As far as Tim's health went, I hoped maybe we could get help from the University of Washington, or maybe even the military. There had to be a program out there that would help people in this situation. I mean, this is America; you can't just let someone die because they don't have health care or any money...right? In the back of my mind I thought I knew the answer to that.

Finally I got up, knocked the frost off the waffles and popped them in the toaster oven. I poured myself another cup of black coffee and sat back down at the round oak table and waited.

It was early afternoon when the phone rang.

A man's voice asked; "Mr. Williams? Sonny Williams?"

"Yes?"

"Are you related to Tim Williams?"

My blood went cold. "Yes, he's my brother, why?"

"Well, he's been in an accident. Right now he's in the hospital in critical condition.

The police found him in a rolled over pickup truck at the bottom of Magnolia Hill. I'm sorry, but it doesn't look good."

I got the name of the hospital and was out the door.

At the hospital a nurse took me to a window of the critical care ward. I wouldn't have recognized Tim if they hadn't told me it was him. He was lying in bed with bandages covering half his face. The other half of his face was swollen and discolored. He had IV`s hanging everywhere. I couldn't speak.

When I finally recovered enough to talk, I turned to the nurse and asked, "What happened? Is he gonna make it?" I felt tears running down my face and into my mouth.

Before the nurse could answer, a voice behind us said, "Excuse me, Mr. Williams? I'm Doctor Gatski. If you'll follow me to my office I'll try and answer your questions."

I followed the doctor down the hall and into a small office no bigger than a cubicle. He motioned me towards a beige plastic chair that had seen better days. He sat down behind a metal desk and looked me straight in the eyes.

"I'll be honest with you," he began. My heart sank. "Your brother has suffered a traumatic head injury as well as internal injuries apparently from the car accident. I can't really tell you too much about the accident, you'll have to talk to the police about that, but I can tell you your brother's injuries are life threatening. He was semi-conscious when he was brought in to emergency but of course he's heavily sedated now. We have stabilized the swelling on his brain for the time being and will continue to monitor the internal hemorrhaging. The next forty-eight hours are critical. If conditions worsen we'd like your permission to operate."

His voice now seemed to be coming out of a fog.

"Mr. Williams? Mr. Williams we'd like your permission to…"

"I'm sorry, yes, of course, do whatever you have to."

"Also I need to ask you, hmm…does your brother have medical insurance?"

"No", I answered weakly.

The doctor looked away and began moving papers around on his desk. "Well, rest assured we'll do all we can for your brother. I believe his personal effects are still in emergency admittance. You may pick them up there if you'd like."

I still had a hundred questions to ask but sensed I was being dismissed so I got up and headed for the door. Before I walked out, I stopped and turned around. "I just want you to know that I'll find a way to take care of the bill."

He just nodded and went back to his papers.

In the emergency ward I found a nurse that was on duty when Tim was brought in. I knew she really didn't have time to talk to me but I wanted to know if she could add anything to what the doctor had already told me. After condolences she did tell me that Tim had been struggling to say something when he was wheeled in.

"He kept saying your name, then something that sounded like …*olden*…or maybe...*old man*. Then he said *mongolia,* or something like that. I'm sorry but that's all I remember. We were pretty busy cutting off his clothes and getting him cleaned up."

"Sure, I understand. I appreciate all you've done. Thanks."

"Oh, another thing, and maybe I shouldn't be saying this but, his clothes…well, they really smelled of alcohol. Almost as if they'd been soaked in it."

CHAPTER THIRTY-ONE

For the next two days I stayed at the hospital and prayed. I prayed for Tim and I prayed that it wouldn't make any difference to anyone that he didn't have medical insurance.

And of course I thought about what Tim was trying to say when he was admitted to the hospital. I was pretty sure he'd found the old man. Now I wanted desperately to drive up to Magnolia and see if I could find him myself but I was afraid to leave the hospital. I thought about what I'd do if I found the guy. I visualized holding him upside down and shaking him until every dollar he had fell out, then sitting on him until he coughed up a hundred thousand or so. I could also see myself walking into Dr. Gatski`s office and dumping a bunch of money on his desk saying,"Okay, here. Now, fix my brother."

While I waited at the hospital, I called the police for their report on the accident. What they told me was unsettling. They said they'd responded to a call from a neighbor in the Magnolia Hill area that reported seeing an over-turned truck at the bottom of a ravine. When officers arrived on the scene, they found a `68 yellow Dodge pickup upside down. It appeared to have been rolled several times. They discovered a Caucasian male inside the cab who appeared to be severely injured. There were several empty beer cans and a broken bottle of scotch inside the cab. The report went on to say the probable cause of the accident was most likely alcohol related. I wasn't so sure of the report but one thing I was sure of...Tim hated scotch.

The hours continued to drag on at the hospital. Tim's condition stayed the same but mine didn't. I was slowly fading. Finally the doctor in charge convinced me to go home and get some rest.

I had every intention of driving straight home from the hospital but as I got behind the wheel I realized that I wouldn't be able to rest until I at least went by the scene of the accident. Something wasn't quite right about the whole thing.

With the help of the police report I drove to the street below the ravine. There was enough daylight left to see where it all happened. Yellow tape marked an area where tall grasses were matted down and littered with broken glass. There were oil stains and a faint smell of gasoline. Looking up I could see the trail of bent and broken branches indicating where he went off the road. I poked around for a while then decided to check out the neighborhood. Maybe a neighbor saw something.

I drove up to the street directly above the ravine and saw a row of expensive looking houses with immaculate lawns and flowerbeds. Even the sidewalks and driveways were spotless. There weren't many vehicles parked along the curb but I figured the homeowners probably had all their cars tucked away inside their perfect two and three car garages.

I parked in the middle of the block and walked up to the house that I thought would have the best view of the gully below. I pushed the doorbell button and immediately heard a melodious chime that went on longer than seemed necessary. Finally a distinguished looking lady with perfectly coiffed silver hair answered the door. "Yes, may I help you?"

Behind her I caught a glimpse of four or five other ladies sitting at a table, playing cards.

"I'm sorry to bother you, but my bother was involved in an accident in the gulley behind your house a couple of nights ago, and I was wondering if you saw or heard anything?"

"Oh my, that was your brother? I'm so sorry! I heard that someone went off the canyon road again. Is he all right?"

"He's … he's in critical condition, but..."

"I'm sorry to hear that. But no, I didn't hear or see anything." Then she peered over her bifocals at me. "They should fix that road. It's a death trap."

"Helen! It's your bid."

"I'm coming! I'm sorry, was there anything else?"

I made two other house calls but got the same results. *Nope, sorry, didn't hear anything.*

At that point I decided to take the doctors advice and go home and get some rest. I got back in my truck and drove slowly down the length of the block and took a left at the next corner. The street was almost identical to the first except for one thing: in front of the third house from the corner, there was a brown Chevy pickup parked at the curb. My adrenaline picked up when I drove closer to the truck and noticed lettering on the side: "Panamco International Oil Field Services." I pulled over and tried to gather my thoughts. I was dead tired and had trouble coming up with any kind of game plan. I knew I should probably go home, sleep on it, and come back later. Finally I decided what the hell, I'm here.

I picked the house closest to the pickup, walked up a twisting walkway and rang the bell. I still had no idea what I was going to say and was half hoping no one would answer. The door opened, but the man who answered stayed in the shadow of the entry. It was hard to make out his features.

"Um...hi, my name's Sonny Williams. I'm sorry to bother you but my brother was involved in an accident near here and I was hoping maybe someone saw what happened."

"No, I'm sorry, I can't help you." The man tried to close the door, but I thrust out my foot. This conversation wasn't over.

"Do you know my brother, his name is Tim Williams?"

The man hesitated a beat before answering. "No, why should I know him?"

"Well, I think he was on his way here to see you."

"Why would he do that?"

"Is that your truck out there?"

"Look, I told you, I didn't hear or see anything, now if you'll excuse me…"

As he began to swing the door closed, a shaft of light caught him just enough for me to get a good look at him. I couldn't place him but I knew I'd seen him before. Exhaustion was really setting in as I made my way back to my truck and climbed into the cab. I sat there staring at the house trying to remember how I knew the man. As I started to drive off, I noticed something in his driveway, something out of place for such a pristine neighborhood. There were tiny drops of fresh oil in his driveway.

The Big Dripper.

CHAPTER THIRTY-TWO

I woke up the next morning with a mental hangover. I must have slept, but not soundly. The oil stains had convinced me that I was on Tim's trail but the lingering image of the man in the doorway had played through my mind like a familiar melody that I couldn't place.

I climbed in the shower and let the warm water slowly wash the cobwebs away. As I stood there, I thought about the last three months or so and what I would give to have never set foot on the *Intrepid*. I thought back to the first time in San Francisco when I saw the boat and remember thinking how ugly she was. I thought about the day we pulled away from the pier... *Wait!. That's it! That's where I saw the man before!! The man that tossed our lines! He's the same guy that opened the door to the house in Magnolia! Holy shit!*

I dressed in a hurry and was out the door in under ten minutes. On the drive to the hospital I prayed Tim would be better. I couldn't wait to tell him what I'd put together.

My excitement turned to utter despair when I got to the hospital. Doctor Gatski had seen me coming down the hall and asked me to step into his office where he gave me the bad news; Tim had slipped into a coma and was now on life support. He wasn't expected to live through the night.

It felt like my breath was leaving through every pore in my body and I couldn't breathe. I slumped in a chair as the tears rolled down my face. I vaguely heard the doctor consoling me and saying something about why they couldn't operate, how they'd done all they could. He said I could stay in his office as long as I needed and then he quietly left the room. I was numb.

I don't know how long I stayed weighted down in that chair. Maybe five minutes, maybe an hour. When I finally got myself together, I made my way down to Tim's room. The nurse that was sitting beside him got up and said she'd be right outside if I needed her.

I don't need you, I need my brother!

I stayed with Tim through the night.

Death came in the morning.

I sleepwalked to the parking lot and got in my truck. I laid my head on the steering wheel and it all came gushing out again. I felt like I was throwing up my soul. I howled so hard that I didn't notice the horn blaring. Finally I sensed someone at my window and when I raised my head, the noise stopped.

"Are you all right?" It was one of the nurses from the hospital.

I took a deep breath and nodded. I rolled the window down the rest of the way and forced out, "Yes, thank you. I'll…I'll be okay."

As she walked away I thought I slumped back over the wheel. *Nothing was remotely close to being okay.*

CHAPTER THIRTY-THREE

The next few days my body functioned with no help from my mind. I moved around in a daze, like a robot in slow motion. Through it all I could hear a familiar voice lying to the staff at the hospital about paying the bill. I could hear a distant voice making arrangements for cremation. I could hear that same voice lying to the mortuary director about payment for services about to be rendered. My lips were moving and I was talking but my soul was lifeless. Then, while I was dictating the obituary to a man from the newspaper, I heard a different voice that slapped me awake. It was a male voice, but it wasn't mine.

"Would you care to say how your brother died?"

"What?

"Well, you know...the accident."

"Accident? It wasn't an accident."

"Oh, I'm sorry, I misunderstood. I thought your brother was---"

A surge of energy flew through me and I sat up straight, suddenly awake and alert.

"My brother was murdered."

"Murdered? Oh, I'm sorry. What do you want to do? About the obituary I mean."

Half-listening as the poor man continued to fumble and stutter, I stood and headed for the door. "Yeah, a, listen...just write the good stuff, okay? Leave the part out about how he died."

I left the mortuary and headed for Magnolia. This time I wasn't leaving until I had some answers.

When I got to Magnolia, the oil-field services truck was gone and no one answered the door. I parked my truck across the street and wondered what do next. It had only been a week since Tim had died and I knew I wasn't thinking clearly.

While I sat there, I thought about how I needed to make a decision about a lawyer soon. I thought about putting the house on the market.

I thought about putting a bullet through my brain.

Then I saw the truck coming down the street.

The man gave no indication that he saw me as he pulled up to the curb. When he got out of his truck I could see he was a little taller than I remembered. He was about my height but about twenty years older. His hair was gray and cropped short. He looked reasonably fit...for an *old man*.

I watched as he headed towards the garage door that was automatically opening. He sat a package down on the drive then went inside the empty garage. A minute later he emerged with a garden hose and a long handled brush. He opened up the package and began sprinkling the contents on the oil stain on the driveway.

He had his back to me as I approached him.

"Getting rid of the evidence?" I asked.

He spun around quickly. "What?" Recognizing me he sputtered, "What are you doing here?"

"I was just gonna ask you the same thing. What are *you* doing here? Cleaning up an oil stain?"

"Yeah, that's right. I'm cleaning up an oil stain. In *my* driveway. Now, what are *you* doing on *my* property?"

"Where did this oil stain came from?"

"Probably from my car. Look, I told you I don't know anything about any accident, so---"

"Well, that's probably right. You probably don't know anything about an accident because it wasn't an accident." I was getting louder and closer to him. "I think the oil that you're cleaning up came from my brother's truck. He was here to see you. He was here to see you because you hung me out to dry, me and the other guys on the *Intrepid.* Does that name ring a bell, asshole? The *Intrepid*? I saw you in San Francisco! And I think my brother was here to talk to you about it and now he's dead!"

"Look, I don't know who you are, but you'd better---"

"You don't know me? You don't know who I am? I was so close to him I was spitting on him. "That's funny, cause I know who you are! You're the sonofabitch they call the old man! And I'm pretty goddamn sure you had something to do with my brother's death!"

He looked quickly up and down the neighborhood and held up a hand.

"Okay, okay…let's get off the street."

He turned and headed into the garage. I followed right behind him.

He stopped in the middle of the garage and turned to me. "Look, a...I'm, I'm really sorry about your brother. He should never have come here."

I heard the large overhead garage door closing behind me and I could feel my nerves being stretched even tighter.

"And you're right, your brother's death was no accident," the man said. It was then that I noticed something black and shiny in his hand, and it was pointed right at me.

I lunged at him and grabbed him by the throat. We fell backwards against the wall and then down onto the floor, raining garden tools down on us. As we struggled, I tried to slam his head into the concrete floor. But he was surprisingly strong. I felt one of his hands work up to my face. I felt his thumb bury in below my jawbone followed by excruciating pain. I could feel myself weakening. Then I felt a punch to my side that took all the wind out of me and suddenly I was on my back. The man pounced on me and slammed a shovel handle across my throat. I vainly tried gouging his eyes with my fingers. I began to see black spots in front of his face and felt myself slipping into unconsciousness. Then, everything went dark.

CHAPTER THIRTY-FOUR

I've been knocked unconscious a few times in my life and each time I came to, it was always the same weird feeling: *What happened...where am I?* This time was no different. As my brain drifted back into real time I heard a man cough and clear his throat. I slowly became aware of my own breathing, and images started to take shape as my vision cleared. I was lying on my back on something cold and hard and looking up at rafters. I tried to sit up but couldn't overcome gravity just yet.

"Better lie still for a little bit."

That voice...

Then it all came rushing back. In a panic I tried to sit up again. When that didn't work, I rolled over on to my side and tried to push myself up.

"Hey, take it easy. It's okay."

I looked up at the man that I'd just fought. He bent at the waist with his hands on his knees and asked, "Are you all right?"

My head was throbbing and my Adams apple felt like it had been hit with a hammer but I slowly nodded yes.

"Here, let's get you off the floor," he said, extending a hand.

For a second I thought about trying to grab him again but quickly dismissed it. With his help, I wobbled to my feet.

"Can you talk?" he asked as he let go of my hand.

I rubbed my throat and croaked, "Ye...yeah, I think so."

"Good. Listen, I'm sorry about all this. Come on, let's go in the house."

As he led me out of the garage through a breezeway and into the house, I realized I was still pretty unstable on my feet. I gladly accepted the stuffed chair he offered in his living room while he headed for the kitchen for some water. While I waited, I massaged my throat and tried to blink the fog away. I heard the sound of cupboards being opened and closed, then running water. When he returned he handed me a glass and said, "I've got something stronger but we should probably start with this."

He sat down, and we studied each other for several seconds. Weakly I raised my glass and took a drink. Or at least I tried to. My throat still hurt like hell and it took a couple of tries to swallow without coughing. Finally I got a few sips down and felt the pain in my head fading a little.

"First of all son, let's agree not to do what we just did anymore." The man grimaced, and rubbed the back of his head. "You `bout caved my head in."

"Yeah, well, you surprised me too," I said as I drained the last of the water. "I have a feeling this wasn't the first, er,...confrontation you've been in?"

"Well, I have had some training."

"Wait a minute. You had something in your hand. You had a gun didn't you?"

He looked puzzled. "A gun? No..." He gave a short laugh when he realized what I was talking about.

"I was holding my garage door opener... which is now in a million pieces!"

We didn't say anything for a moment or two, and then I broke the silence. "Who are you? Do you know what happened to my brother?"

He sat his glass down, leaned forward, and folded his hands together, looking at the floor. He studied the carpet for so long I wondered if he'd heard my question.

"Who are you?" I repeated. "What happened to..."

He stood up and waved me off. "I heard you son, I heard you."

He took a deep breath then slowly let it out. His body seemed to slump and he sat back down.

"I might as well tell you. This shit has gone on long enough. My name is Alan Jimeen. And yes, some know me as the `old man`. You're also right about your brother's death, it wasn't an accident."

He looked away and paused for a second before continuing. "But a man I deal with, tried to make it look that way."

"What man? Who?"

"A man named Butch Wray."

"Who's Butch Wray?"

Jimeen stared at me then shook his head. "I know I'm taking a big chance here by telling you any of this, but now someone's been killed and I'll have to live with that, knowing I was part of it. I was hoping to get out of this crap before anything like this happened, but tragically, especially for you and your brother, I didn't."

"Who's Butch Wray?" I repeated impatiently.

"Butch Wray is a man who, how shall I put this...*enlisted* me years ago to broker loads of marijuana." Jimeen stopped for a moment. "Ah, the hell with it, Butch Wray is a man that's been blackmailing me for years. The other night he was here and dropped off a satchel full of money. I was in the garage about to put it in my floor safe when I heard someone drive up. I figured it was Wray again and he'd forgotten something. That's when your brother showed up. Walked right on in the side door into the garage, almost like he owned the place."

He stopped long enough to take a drink of water then went on, "I didn't know who he was, but he sure as shit seemed to know me. 'Hey, old man, how ya doin`? he said, or something like that."

I could visualize Tim standing in the doorway running a bluff like that.

"I asked him what he wanted and he said he wanted to know if I was the chicken-shit bastard that was letting his brother rot in jail. I told him I didn't know what he was talkin` about and to get the hell off my property, but he just kept comin` at me, kinda like you did." Jimeen smiled sadly. "Must be in the genes."

I began to feel nauseated.

"Anyway, your brother saw the satchel on the floor and wanted to know what was in it. I didn't say anything and he went to pick it up. I grabbed him and spun him around and we started to get into it. Well, I didn't know it right then but Wray *had* forgotten something and had come back. He must have heard the noise in the garage because he opened the side door and came up behind your brother. I didn't see the shovel in his hand until it was too late. He...he hit your brother in the head, and when he fell, his head hit hard on the concrete floor. Wray bent over him and checked his pulse, and, well, he said he was dead. That was it."

Jimeen stopped to clear his throat, then looked me in the eye and said, "I'm sorry, I really am."

"How do I know you're telling the truth? How do I know it wasn't you who killed him?"

"Good question." He seemed to be considering whether he should say anymore. Finally he stood up and said, "Wait here." He was gone about a minute and when he came back he waved a small black plastic cartridge in his right hand. "Wray has a thing about security cameras and insisted I install a couple around my house. This cartridge came from the camera I had mounted in the entry, the one that's aimed at the side door of the garage. You'll only see twelve seconds before the door closes, but that should be enough."

He was right about the twelve seconds, they were more than enough. The video left me trembling. The scene played out just as Jimeen had said, but now I knew what my brother's killer looked like. Wray`s face was thin and pock-marked. He had black, greasy looking hair that hung over his eyes. It was hard to guess his age on the black and white film, but I put it at about forty-five.

"You ready for something stronger now?" Jimeen asked as he picked up my water glass.

"Yeah...please."

Jimeen went to the kitchen and came back with two glasses filled halfway with an amber colored liquid.

"So, how`d my brother get to the bottom of the ravine?" I asked. "You guys load him up and roll him down the hill?"

"I didn't...but apparently Wray did."

"What do you mean, *apparently?*"

"When Wray told me your brother was dead, I told him I was going to call an ambulance, but Wray got pissed and said, `Don't call anyone, gimme a minute to think.`"

I could feel a rage building inside me. The thought of my brother lying on the garage floor while some asshole thought about what to do with his body was almost too much to comprehend.

The image gave way to Jimeen`s voice again. "Finally, Wray says he'll take care of everything, all I gotta do is bring him whatever liquor I have in the house. Then he suggested I go down to the bowling alley and let people see me down there. Told me to stay there 'til after midnight at least. So I did, and when I came back, your brother and his truck were gone. It was like nobody had been here, like nothing had happened.

"I know you have no reason to believe me, but I swear if I would have known your brother was still alive, I would have helped him, Butch Wray, or no Butch Wray."

I stared at him for a long time, neither one of us saying anything. Finally I said, "Okay, where is Wray now?"

"I'm not sure I can tell you that just yet."

"Bullshit!" I had gotten to my feet and was starting to lose it again. "What's stopping me from going to the cops right now? I mean it! You've got that tape! You can see what happens! And *you're* involved. Just because you didn't do the actual killing doesn't mean you're any less responsible! You better tell me what I want to know, goddamn it! I don't have a fuckin` thing to lose anymore. In fact I'd probably get a nice little reduced sentence if I tell the feds about you and this Wray guy!"

Jimeen held up his hands. "Look, I can't imagine what you're going through right now, but please, listen. Yes, you could go to the cops or the feds or whoever right now, and yeah, you could probably swing a deal, maybe be out of prison in a few years. But there's a good chance if you do that, Wray could get away scot-free!"

I cooled just enough to ask what the hell he was talking about.

"Your name's Sonny, right?"

I nodded.

"Well Sonny, you might think this tape is all you need, but think about it; a sharp lawyer could claim your brother was attacking me and Wray just came to my defense. He could argue that your brother was drunk when he came here, and left with a sore head. Nothing on this tape shows what happened after the door closed. A lawyer would have this evidence dismissed in a minute. I let you see it to show I was telling you the truth. Besides, this tape goes in the fireplace as soon as you leave this house."

I stopped and looked at him. "You wouldn't do that..."

"I would, and I will. Don't mess with me. And as far as me testifying, you can forget it. Sonny, believe me when I tell you, this man has me by the balls. I have a lot to lose. More than you know."

"Then why are you telling me anything at all?"

"I'm not quite sure yet, but there's something else you might wanna know about Wray."

"Yeah, what?" I said as I sat back down.

"He's the reason you went to jail. He set you up."

"He did what? What're you talking about?"

"He had someone plant a transmitter on your boat so the feds could find you. He sent an anonymous letter with the frequency of the device and told `em the *Intrepid* was coming in loaded with pot."

The mention of *someone* planting a bug rubbed a raw nerve, but the fact that Wray was behind it all really hit another one.

And then another thought suddenly occurred to me, *is Kelli mixed up with this guy?*

"Wait a minute," I said. "I know all about the bug being planted, but why would Wray do it? I thought he was involved in all this."

"He is. In fact he's the main man as far as I know. You see, Sonny, while the coast guard was tracking you guys, Wray slipped a bigger load through. Ran an end-around if you will."

"A *bigger* load? We had over seventeen tons on the *Intrepid!* And according to the news report, it was worth over fifty million dollars! Can this guy afford to lose that much?"

Jimeen looked at me and shrugged,"Yeah, well maybe it would have been worth that much by the time it was all broken down and distributed, but all Wray was out was the two-hundred thousand that he paid for the load, I know because I took the money over to Thailand for him. Of course to the guy in the Thailand jungle the two-hundred grand was a fortune, but to Wray, it was just the cost of insurance on the other load that he ran through, which by the way, was worth twice as much as what you guys had. You probably noticed that the *Intrepid* wasn't in the best of shape? The boat was expendable, a write-off, and as far as Wray was concerned, so were you and the crew."

I couldn't control myself any longer and I jumped back up. "Goddamn that son-of a-bitch! God*damn* him!" I pointed my finger at Jimeen. "You listen to me now. I want that bastard. You tell me where he is right fucking now or I'm going straight to the D.E.A!"

Jimeen held up a hand. "Okay, okay, just settle down for a minute."

I took a deep breath and calmed a little, and then said, "I want this man. I don't give a goddamn about anything anymore, just him. I'll give you my word I won't say anything about you, just tell me where he is."

Jimeen looked at me for a long time before he spoke. "You're really serious aren't you?"

"Of course I'm serious, Where is he?"

"Well, right now Wray is in Malaysia putting a deal together for another boatload of pot. I carried the money over for him."

"When will he be back?"

"Hard to say for sure, he's also overseeing an engine overhaul on a ship in Singapore. Once that's done he plans to bring that ship back to the States. He'll be hauling some oil drilling equipment that I brokered for an outfit in California. Everything legit as far as I know. I think they're putting the final touches to the boat as we speak."

"Well, that doesn't do me much good, now does it? I'll probably be back in jail before he gets back here."

"Maybe there is a way I can help."

"I'm listening."

"Once Wray leaves Singapore, Wray and a local crew will sail east to Labuan to pick up his cargo and take on fuel."

"Labuan? He's going to Labuan?"

"Yeah, if you're sailing east from Singapore, Labuan is one of the last places in Malaysia to get fuel before going through the Philippines and into the Pacific. Well, you know that, right? You guys were there."

"Yeah, that's right." I said bitterly.

"Well, before Wray leaves Labaun, he'll change crew. There'll be four people on the boat counting Wray. One of the crew is already over there and he'll be the cook and help stand watches. I'm sending the first mate, who doubles as a radioman, over in about a two weeks."

Again he paused and seemed to be considering whether to go on or not.

"So?" I prodded.

"So….he's also expecting me to send him an engineer."

"Yeah, and…?"

Jimeen shrugged. "He's never seen you before has he?"

It took a moment to register.

I looked Jimeen straight in the eye and asked,"You mean you'll send *me* over there? You'll get me on his boat so, so…I'll take care of him? Toss him overboard or something? For you? Is that right?"

"*You* wanted him," Jimeen said, annoyed. "Look, I'm not going to sit here and lie to you and say his death wouldn't benefit me as well, but what you do with him is your business."

I sat there stunned for a moment, then I said, "Aren't you forgetting something? I'm out on bail right now. I don't have a passport. Even if I wanted to, how in the hell would I get out of here?"

"Let's just say I have the resources to get you a passport and out of the country. We'd need to change your appearance a little. It looks like you got a couple of days growth on your face now. I'd let it grow."

My head was spinning again. This was all coming way too fast."Look," I began, suddenly feeling very tired, "I've had my life tossed upside down in the last six months. I took the job on the *Intrepid* to try and get my brother out of the jam he was in. I had no intention of doin` more than just the one trip. It was a stupid, but sometimes a man does stupid things to protect his family. I thought I was going to die on that boat more than once. Then I find out that I was probably suckered by someone that I thought loved me. Right now I don't know if I can trust anybody again."

I took a breath and said, "And I don't know what's going on here for sure. I need to back away from this for right now. And, well, I…a…I need to bury my brother."

"I know. I understand," Jimeen said. "You take care of what you need to, and again, I'm really sorry." He didn't say anything for a moment, and then added, "Just think about what I said. It's your call. If you do decide to travel, let me know as soon as you can. There's arrangements that I have to make right away."

I left Jimeens house thinking about the arrangements I had made for Tim. I wondered if Jimeen was doing the same for me.

CHAPTER THIRTY-FIVE

I hired a captain with a forty-foot classic Criss Craft to take my brothers` ashes out on the waters of Puget Sound near Seattle. I had brought a tape player and music with me, music that my brother and I both loved. I was doing okay until the lyrics of one of the songs hit me. I was reduced to a puddle. I felt grief so deeply that I thought my body and spirit would break into pieces and I would simply cease to exist. I would be no more. I waited for it to happen, wanting it to happen.

But my body didn't quit. I kept breathing.

After a while I felt the hand of the captain on my shoulder, and I slowly I looked up to see dolphins darting in and out of the wake behind us. It was a comforting sight, as if they'd tasted my tears and were trying to console me. I straightened enough to salute them and my brother, and then I told the captain to head for shore.

Two days later I was going over all the letters I had received from different attorneys since I'd been out on bail. Most of them read about the same: "Retain me and I *might* be able to get you eight to ten years, and with good behavior you could be out in…blah, blah, blah. Only fifty thousand dollars! But hurry, this offer won't last!"

This was all very depressing so I shoved the letters aside. I wondered if what I knew about Jimeen and Wray would be enough to make a deal for a reduced sentence. In the short time that I had been in jail I found out what they did to rats or snitches that turned state`s evidence, but I didn't care. I wouldn't hesitate to tell the feds about Wray, but for some reason I didn't feel that way about Jimeen. There was something about him that made me wonder why he was in this business at all.

The phone rang and I picked it up. Speak of the devil. Jimeen spoke quickly, "Sonny I thought I should tell you, the schedule has been moved up. We need to move fast on this. Have you made up your mind?"

"I don't know yet. I'm still sorting things out."

"Anything I can help you with?"

One of the things that bothered me was the hold that Wray seemingly had on Jimeen. Was Jimeen as dirty as Wray? Was I being set up again? I didn't want to be stepping into something I couldn't finish. I wanted more details.

"Yeah, I'd like to know how you got involved in all of this in the first place. I wanna know what this guy has on you."

My question was met with silence for a minute. "Okay, that's fair, but I don't want to talk about it over the phone. Can you come over now?"

"I'm on my way."

Jimeen answered the door on my first knock. "Hey, Sonny, come on in." As he led me into his living room he asked, "Wanna drink? Coffee or something?"

"No thanks." I wasn't in the mood for pleasantries, but I *was* in the mood for some answers. As I sat down, it occurred to me that Jimeen hadn't said anything about a wife or family. "You live here alone?"

"Yeah, my wife died three years ago. It's just me now."

"She know what you did for a living?" I asked, maybe a little too sarcastically.

"I assume you're wondering if my wife knew about my involvement with Wray or any of the other shit, and the answer is no. All she knew was that I worked in the oil field service business. Still do."

"So how`d you hook up with Wray?"

Jimeen drew in a deep breath and said, "Okay, I might as well tell you, a short version anyway. Years ago when I was first married, I was a buyer for Richfield Marine International. I brokered deals for oil field equipment: drill pipe, pumps, heavy equipment, whatever they might need out in the field, or at sea for that matter. In fact, I put the deal together for the equipment that Wray's about to bring back. Anyway, with my job I could travel in and out of countries fairly easy. I also carried a lot of money with me to expedite quick transactions, saving both the buyer and seller quite a bit of money. Well, on one of my trips overseas, I met a woman and fell in love with her. Later we had a child together. A beautiful daughter. Of course I didn't tell my wife about it. Looking back on it I can see why I was a candidate for blackmail.

"My wife was deeply involved with some wonderful charities and was well respected in the community. She was even considering entering into some grass roots political stuff. Unfortunately, early on in our marriage we found out she couldn't have children and she had a hard time dealing with that. We sorta drifted apart, but she was a good person and I didn't want to see her get hurt."

Watching Jimeen tell his story, I couldn't tell if I was watching a very good actor that had his own agenda, or a sincere man that was telling the truth. He took a moment and seemed to be gathering his thoughts before continuing.

"When Wray first approached me, he asked me to deliver some cash to some people in Thailand. How he got my name I don't know, apparently he had people looking for someone like me. I had just started my own business and wanted no part of him. That's when he threatened to tell my wife about my little affair. He said if I just carried some money one time for him, he would disappear from my life. `*One and done*`, he said. Of course that's never the case with blackmailers. Once you do something for `em, they got you. Well, after my wife died, I figured I could get away from the scumbag, but he came up with another way to blackmail me. Besides, I was screwed from the very first deal. I'm in too deep now."

"So you're hoping I go whack this asshole for you, huh?"

"Well, Sonny, again, that's up to you. You're sitting in a bad place. I can't stop you from going to the cops with everything that I've told you, and maybe that's the right play for you. You could get a good lawyer and maybe make a deal. But the thing is, you're still going to do time, and Wray probably won't. And you and I both know how they treat snitches in prison. I'm sure they'd offer you protection, but once the word is out in jail that you turned other people in to save your own butt...well, you're sitting in a bad place right now."

Thoughts of Kelli and Wray began to burn in my brain.

"One way or another Sonny, I gotta know. You wanna go?"

I took a deep breath and said, "Yes, I do. I *need* to go."

"You know once you leave..."

"Yeah, yeah I know."

Jimeen looked at me for a moment. "Okay, you'll need to go downtown and get a passport picture taken. Any of those places on First Avenue will do. And cut your hair. Get a crew cut or one of those buzz cuts. We need to change your appearance as much as possible. Try and get it done by Friday so I can get working on the passport. The passport should take about a week. Soon as I get the passport taken care of, I'll make the travel arrangements and let Wray know that you're coming. Do you care what your new name will be? On the passport I mean."

I shrugged. "No, I don't care. I hadn't thought about it."

"Okay, let's see ...how `bout ...Jack...Jack Tatcher, or something like that?"

"Yeah, that's fine, whatever."

"Alright. Have you hired a lawyer or been given a sentencing date yet?"

"No."

"Good, I'll try and get you out of the country within two weeks. You'll have to really keep a low profile in the meantime. Try not to talk with too many people but go through any legal motions the courts ask of you, short of going back to jail of course."

"Of course."

"Uh…you have any more questions?"

"Yeah, since you're hiring me, I'd like some money up front. I'll need some traveling money. I'd also like to pay for my brother's expenses before I go." I figured if Jimeen was willing to put me on the trail of his partner, then he'd be willing to pay for it. Whatever the outcome might be. To my relief Jimeen said, "Sure, I understand. How much do you need?"

I naively said, "Twenty thousand should do it."

"Fine, no problem. When you bring me your passport pictures, I'll have the money for you."

After I left Jimeens` I thought about how this whole situation had changed in a few short months. I had just negotiated for a one way ticket out of the country I had honorably served so I could catch up to the man who had killed my brother. To do what? Kill him? Just as every fiber in my soul wanted Wray, I was already wondering if I could become a killer. And what about Kelli? What would I do if I saw her again?

I guess I was about to find out.

CHAPTER THIRTY-SIX

"Sir? Excuse me...Mr. Tatcher?" The words drifted through my thoughts over the quiet hum of jet engines. A jolt went through me and I sat up straight. A smiling stewardess was leaning in toward my seat at the window.

"Sir, would you like something to drink with your meal?"

"Oh...a...yeah sure" I stammered. "An orange juice please." I had been lost in thought ever since I had boarded the plane in Seattle. The last two weeks had been a torment for me. I hadn't slept much worrying about if I was doing the right thing. Jimeen had kept his word by supplying me with money to pay off Tim's expenses, in fact he added another five thousand to help me get started in my new life. But I worried someone would spot my phony passport. I worried that I'd get caught trying to leave the country. But most of all, I worried that if I didn't go after Butch Wray myself, he would get away with killing my brother.

Now, there was no turning back. I was on an airplane heading for Hong Kong. I would connect there for a flight to Kota Kinabula Malaysia, then to the island of Labuan, or as the ticket agent had cheerfully called it, "my final destination." His words were not lost on me. I knew I was headed for some sort of finality. In any case, I was now a wanted fugitive, and at best, that's what I would be for the rest of my life. Like it or not, the rough plan I had worked out to deal with Wray was now in motion.

As I looked out the window, I had to be honest and admit that a big part of my decision to run was based on the possibility of seeing Kelli again. I wanted to confront her. I wanted to know for certain if she planted the tracking device. But I also knew that if she was connected with Wray, I couldn't just show up on her doorstep without setting off alarms. If what Jimeen had told me was true, I'd have a couple of days on the island of Labuan before Wray would arrive and I was hoping that my new hair color and beard would keep me from being recognized by some of the people I'd met before.

If I could get a corner room on about the third or forth floor of the Labuan Hotel, I could keep an eye on arriving ships in the harbor. I would also have a view of the rear of the hospital where Kelli had her apartment. I might need a pair of binoculars, but I could see who came and went. I'd probably feel like a peeping-tom but it would give me a chance to study things from a safe distance. If Kelli was involved with Wray, he'd show up at her place at some point.

My thoughts were interrupted again as the stewardess set my meal in front of me. I wasn't really hungry but with time to kill, it gave me something to do. Then a sobering thought crossed my mind: *Time to kill? Hell, I had the rest of my life to kill.*

Sometime later, I handed my empty tray back to the stewardess and settled back in my seat. I began to think my plan through again, but with a full belly I soon dozed off. In a fitful nap I dreamed about the movie, *The African Queen.* It was one of the last scenes when Humphrey Bogart and Katharine Hepburn were about to be executed on the deck of a German warship. At Bogey's last request, the captain of the ship had married the two and had just slipped nooses around Bogart and Hepburn`s necks. Suddenly it was Kelli and Wray's heads that were in the nooses and I was the captain about to give the command to hang them. All of a sudden the ship started shaking and a warning of some sort carried through the air. I tried to reach Kelli to take the noose off her neck but the bouncing and shaking kept her just out of my reach. The warning sounded again, "...and gentleman, we're experiencing some mild turbulence. The captain has just turned on the seat belt sign. Please return to your seats and keep your seat belts securely fastened."

I opened my eyes to see the stewardess walking down the isle checking seat belts and assuring people that the captain would turn off the seat belt sign as soon as it was safe to do so. Moments later we were in smooth air again. I wondered that if I drifted back to my dream whether I could save Kelli or not. I wondered if I wanted to.

With nothing else to do for the next twelve hours or so, I went over my plan in my mind again and tried to imagine how things might play out when I'd finally meet up with Wray. I thought about getting a gun and just shooting him in the face the minute I saw him. I wanted to kill Wray, but I also wanted to get away with it.

I remembered from my time in the navy that there were villages scattered around the Philippines that were simpatico to Americans soldiers and sailors who had changed their minds about fighting in the Viet Nam war. My plan was simple. I would assume the role as engineer and stay aboard the *Gladiator* until we got close to the Philippines. Then during the night when Wray was at the helm and the rest of the crew were asleep, I would smash Wray on the head with something very heavy, then toss him overboard. While the sharks were introducing themselves to Wray, I'd set the autopilot and then escape in a life raft. If my luck held, I'd be on a beach near one of those villages when the rest of the crew woke up somewhere in the Pacific.

CHAPTER THIRTY-SEVEN

I had a two-day layover in Hong Kong so I grabbed a cheap hotel in Kowloon. I was hoping I could rest up and sleep off my jet lag, but after hours of tossing and turning, I eventually gave up and took a ferry to downtown Hong Kong.

I had been in Hong Kong once before while on R&R from the navy and from what I could see, some things had changed while others had not changed at all. There were still a gazillion people crammed shoulder to shoulder on the island; the ubiquitous taxis bumper to bumper blaring the same tune on their horns; the same scene of headless chickens, ducks and other fowl hanging upside down from hooks in the outdoor market stalls; and all the stench and odors that went with it.

One of the popular hangouts at that time had been a place called Suzie Wongs and I surprised myself by finding it again.

Not much had changed in Suzie's as far as the décor went. Ceiling fans still slowly revolved above the wooden chairs and tables that were scattered around a horseshoe bar. Drab red paint still adorned the walls. A jukebox sat in the corner.

It was early in the evening and there were a few people of mixed nationalities in the place, but not like it was before. Years earlier you would have found young bar girls sitting on U.S. sailor's and soldier's laps, laughing and negotiating prices. Music would be blaring over clinking glasses and shouted drink orders. And there was a feeling that you had come to a place where you could forget your troubles for a while.

Now, Suzie's felt somewhat subdued. Maybe it was the price of the Paris Peace talks.

As I sat down at the bar I noticed there were still a few working girls scattered at different tables. It wasn't long before two giggling girls approached me.

"Short-time, good-time, Joe?" one of them asked.

They frowned and turned up their noses when I waved them off, but I noticed they quickly regained their smiles while they bounced over to a couple of sailors that had just strolled in.

Suddenly out of nowhere a voice snapped me awake. "Hey, Sonny."

Holy shit! I jumped and quickly turned to see who was behind the voice. It was a middle-aged Chinese woman with a crooked smile.

"You no like young girls? You like me betta, maybe?"

"Oh, no, a …a…thanks, but no, no thanks."

I was stammering but relived that she wasn't calling me by my name. *I've got to remember that my name is not Sonny. I'm Jack. Jack Tatcher.*

"Maybe you like young boys then. I fix you up, yes?"

"No, please, it's okay… really."

"You not happy man, yes?"

I took a couple of dollars from my change on the bar and handed them to her. "Ah…look, I just want to be left alone, okay?"

She took my money, gave me a funny look and said, "You wan be alone?"

"Yes."

"Then why you here?"

Back at my hotel, I showered and crawled into bed. Again I had trouble getting to sleep. The woman's words from Suzie's rolled through my head. *You not happy man, yes?*

She had me there. I thought of Wray. *Would killing him make me happy?* No, I doubted it, but it might bring me some sort of satisfaction and at this point in my life, it seemed it was all

I had to live for. I wondered if anything would ever make me happy again. I thought that the worst day of my life was the day Tim had died, but the complete, utter hopelessness I was feeling now was overwhelming. I felt completely alone. I knew that the long flight and lack of sleep was adding to my depression but I couldn't help but understand that, now, not only did I not have any family to return to; I didn't have a country to return to either. I was in effect, homeless and without love in my heart. Mentally and physically exhausted, I finally fell asleep.

I awoke the next morning with a start, and in a flash, reality came crashing in. I realized it was time to stop feeling sorry for myself and get on with whatever lay ahead. The idea that I would be seeing Wray in a couple of days, energized me. The idea that I might be seeing Kelli before the sun went down got me the rest of the way out of bed. It was a new day and I had a new identity. It was time to get on with it.

CHAPTER THIRTY-EIGHT

The flight to Kota Kinabula went smoothly and I cleared customs with no problems as Jack Tatcher. The flights so far had been gratefully uneventful, cruising well above everything at thirty thousand feet, but the final leg of my trip was in a much smaller plane that fairly skimmed over the top of the tropical forests of eastern Malaysia. I was amazed at how vast the green jungle was; it seemed to stretch on forever without any breaks in its canopy. I contemplated about how easy it would be for someone to get lost and disappear down there. The thought was appealing.

After cruising over the jungle for about twenty minutes we broke out over the sea. I could see several ships and the wakes they were leaving as they made their way in all directions. The thought crossed my mind that I might be looking at Wray`s ship.

Minutes later the aircraft banked slowly to the left and on the horizon I could see the island of Labuan. I could also see the oil tankers anchored a few miles from the island. I wondered if anybody was having a "jolly" on any of them. *Was Kelli down there?* As we drew closer, I could make out the harbor and town. Soon I was able to spot the beige colored, seven-story Labuan hotel. I could also see the gleaming white hospital building next to the hotel. My palms began to sweat.

The tropical heat blasted me as I stepped off the plane and walked across the tarmac towards the terminal. When I entered the small airport building, something else hit me: I was now in the part of the world where the next person I bumped into, could be Kelli…or Wray.

The terminal was slightly air-conditioned but as I stood at the baggage claim looking at the faces around me, I could feel the sweat rolling down my back. I was also scratching at my new beard, beginning to wonder if I could get used to it, especially in the tropical heat. I don't know how long I stood there looking at every woman that walked by but I finally realized there was only one bag left to claim…mine.

I grabbed my bag and headed outside. There weren't many cars around and I looked for something that resembled a taxi or a bus. Across the road from the terminal I could see a guy leaning against a car reading a newspaper. There was something familiar about him. Fighting an urge to turn and go the other way, I took a few steps closer, trying to remember where I knew him. Before I could look away he glanced up from his paper and saw me. A big smile spread across his face when he saw me. "Hey, you wan` ride to town?"

Then it hit me. It was Hector, the guy that gave me and Kelli a ride to the leeward side of the island.

"Ah...yeah, sure," I said. He quickly folded his paper, opened the back door then hurried over to me.

"This all?" he asked as he picked up my sea bag.

"Yeah, that's it."

"You sailor man?" he asked as he put my bag in the trunk.

"Yeah, I'm sailor man…why?" I asked the question casually as I settled in the back seat. He didn't answer until we had pulled away from his parking spot, then I caught his eyes looking at me in the rear view mirror. "I know you," he said. "You `Merikan sailor right?"

"Yes," I answered. My nerves were on full alert now, sweat beading on my forehead.

"You Popeye!" he said gleefully. "You Popeye the sailor man!"

I chuckled.

"You wan` tour of island? I drive you, maybe yes?"

His eyes caught mine in the mirror again. I shook my head and said, "Nah, that's okay."

For a moment I was tempted to ask him if he knew a shortcut into town just to see his reaction.

"My name Hector. You need anything, you call Hector, okay-dokay?"

"Sure, Hector. By the way, my name is Jack, Jack Tatcher."

As we pulled up to the hotel entrance, I noticed two men in military uniforms standing on either side of the glass entry doors. Again I felt the sweat trickling down my back. Hector quickly opened my door and then popped open the trunk and grabbed my bag. As we approached the doors, the men seemed to be checking me out.

Just stay cool. I'm Jack Tatcher and I've done nothing wrong.

Hector said something in Malay and both men nodded, grabbed the door handles and opened the doors for us, ushering us in. I felt the hotel's lobby air-condition wash over me as I made my way to the front desk. I smiled for the second time that day. *Hell yes I'm cool. I'm Jack Tatcher and I've done nothing wrong… yet.*

I asked for, and got, a corner room for the best view of the harbor. Of course it also overlooked Kelli`s apartment nicely. From one set of windows I could see the harbor and the main dock, where not that long ago, the *Intrepid* had been moored. The pier was about half-full of various sized ships, a couple of them I thought I recognized from the last trip. I could see the water taxis shuttling workers back and forth from the quay to the small shipyard across the harbor. Everything was as I remembered it.

From the other corner window I couldn't quite make out the main entrance to the hospital but I could definitely see the backside of it, the side where Kelli had her apartment. Palm trees shaded the entry to her place, but I would be able to see anybody coming or going. I stared down at the round concrete steps leading to her door, the same steps that I had walked across on many delicious nights. I wondered if anybody had been watching me then.

With nothing else to do until dark, I pulled a comfortable looking chair up to the window and settled in. I began to think about what I would do after I killed Wray. The idea of living in the Philippines didn't appeal to me much, although it was still much better than a long prison stretch in America.

Maybe there'd be a chance I could sign on as engineer on a small freighter out of the Philippines and travel around for a while. *Maybe work my way down to Australia?* Australia was appealing for enough reasons but I was also leery of the country's extradition laws and their relationship with the U.S. Maybe it would be better to stay in more of a third world country for the time being. Maybe a country like…Malaysia? The people were friendly and I loved here once. Maybe it could happen again.

I even played out the scenario of riding all the way back with Wray if I missed the opportunity to kill him. But after a moment or two I decided that wasn't an option. Wray would not be aboard the *Gladiator* when it arrived in San Francisco, and neither would I.

I thought about our chances of running into pirates again. Too bad I couldn't call up our adversaries from before: "*Hi there, you might not remember me but we met a few months ago in the South China Sea? Yeah, I'm good, thanks. Say listen, I've got a job you might be interested in …*"

I thought again how much my life had changed in such a short time. It wasn't that long ago I had an honorable navy discharge in my hand and was looking forward to a bright future. Now I was sitting in a hotel room in a foreign country trying to figure out what to do and where to go…after I *murder* a man.

The chair must have been comfortable, or the traveling had tired me out because I dozed off. When I awoke, the shadows were long against the wall and a growling stomach reminded me I hadn't eaten anything since early that morning. I stood up, stretched and looked at Kelli`s place for a few more minutes. Nobody came or went and with a glance through the other window, I could tell the activity at the pier hadn't changed; no new ships had tied up. I went in the bath and splashed some water in my face. I couldn't be sure if the face in the mirror still looked like Sonny Williams or not. I decided it was as good a time as ever to see if there was anybody in the hotel bar and restaurant that I might remember, or more importantly, that might remember me?

As I walked into the hotel bar, one of my questions was soon answered. Ahmad, the bartender that had been with us for the jolly aboard the *Intrepid,* was working. He was wiping down some glasses with his back to the only customer at the bar.

There were only three or four couples at the tables and my first glance told me that Kelli was not among them. I scooted up to the bar and nodded to the other guy sitting three stools down from me.

"Yes sir, may I help you?" Ahmad chirped as he turned to me.

"Yeah, I'd like a rum and coke please."

"Of course."

As Ahmad moved to his left to make my drink, I stole another look at the tables and confirmed that Kelli was not there. Good. I relaxed a little.

When Ahmad delivered my drink, he pushed a plate of peanuts in front of me before excusing himself. I watched as he made his way around the bar and began picking up glasses and taking orders from the couples at the tables. If he remembered me he gave no indication.

I recognized one of the waitresses that had also been aboard the *Intrepid*, but she gave no signs of recognizing me either. I was beginning to gain some confidence in my new look.

After dinner, buoyed by a few drinks and a full belly, I decided a walk into town and down to the wharf wouldn't compromise anything. Then maybe a walk by the hospital just to see if there was a light on in Kelli's apartment.

There wasn't much activity going on in town but I recognized a lot of the same people working, or in most cases, sitting, in the same places they were months earlier. Many of the small restaurants and storefronts were fully open toward the street and as I walked by I could see the proprietors slouched at tables, staring up at flickering black and white televisions on the wall. Some of them gave me a cursory look, and then went back to what they were doing, or not doing.

I turned a corner and saw Mr. Jhan sweeping the stoop in front of his hardware store. He glanced up at me but quickly went back to his business. Scrawny cats seemed to be lying in front of every store in town and when I passed by they gave me weak meows and followed me with their eyes.

Although it was still fairly early, some store owners had already closed for the evening, a steel roll-up garage door pulled down and padlocked, or an accordion steel mesh door stretched across the front of their store. I was pretty much ignored by everyone but the cats.

As I made my way through town I found a store that sold binoculars. When I picked out a pair and offered to pay with U.S. currency, the store owner didn't even blink. He just pulled out a small calculator, jabbed at it then held it up for me to see: sixty-five dollars. I forked over the cash.

When I reached the wharf I counted eight small ships and boats, five on one side and three on the other. It looked like there was room for another two or three more. I made mental notes of the ships` flags as I walked the length of the pier. A real hodgepodge of countries were still represented; China, Bahrain, England, Malay, France, and others.

But no ships with the name *Gladiator*.

Most of the ships were about two hundred feet long and didn't seem to have many crew members aboard. The smaller boats were darkened with no sign of life. I stopped at a cleat that was rusted and loose; I remembered it was where we had tied up the *Intrepid.* It was where Kelli stood the day she brought my towel back to me. I tried shaking off the memory like a dog coming out of water but my mind automatically replayed that scene. She had been so beautiful looking down at me that day. The white blouse and white shorts setting off those golden brown arms and legs. Her dimpled, dazzlingly smile. I felt a stirring in my heart…or was it just my loins?

Some jabbering by some drunken sailors coming down the dock broke my reverie. With nothing more to see on the pier, I turned and headed back towards town.

As I rounded the north end of the hospital, I picked up my pace and walked with my head down as if I were really headed somewhere else. When I got close to Kelli's apartment I allowed myself a quick glance at her place and continued on without breaking stride. There was a light on in the bedroom window. Without looking back, I walked on past a street lamp and into darkness.

I walked for another five minutes on a dirt road until it dead-ended at the edge of the jungle. I turned and headed back, still wondering what the hell I was doing. I walked back past her place with the same purpose in my stride as before, but this time when I glanced up, I saw the light go off. It was bedtime for somebody.

Suddenly, I was feeling very tired myself and decided to call it a night. Tomorrow would be a new day.

Back in my hotel room I slowly undressed and crawled into bed. I wondered if Kelli was asleep yet. I wondered if she was alone.

CHAPTER THIRTY-NINE

I awoke the next morning to the sound of raindrops. After a quick stop in the bathroom I went directly to the front windows. A small rain squall was moving through and my view of the harbor was somewhat obscured, but I could see the wharf and could make out the shapes of the ships. There were still eight of them in the same positions as last night. Through the corner window I could see the tops of palm trees waving in the wind and I watched a few people walking hurriedly along the sidewalk, some running and cutting across the hospital lawn to escape the rain. Something grabbed my eye and I saw movement on the porch at Kelli's apartment...someone was coming out the door!

Whomever it was paused under the entry awning. From my angle, looking down, all I could see was the top of white shoes, legs and the hem of a white dress. I watched while the shoes turned around and went back in the building. I stood there, afraid to move, heart beating faster with each passing moment. Suddenly the shoes were back. They hesitated for a second, then moved out from under the cover. Only another cover came with her...in the form of an umbrella.

I watched as the umbrella moved over the circular steps and then angled towards the sidewalk. Rain rolling down my window blurred my vision, but just before the figure was out of view, a gust of wind blew the umbrella away for a split second, just long enough to expose a shock of short black hair.

I sat in my room for a long time trying to figure out what to do. I knew the smart thing would be to forget about Kelli and hunker down in my room until the *Gladiator* arrived, but since smart hadn't entered into a lot of my thinking lately, I gave up on that idea and headed down to the lobby with something else in mind.

The phone booths were deserted as I slid into one and looked up the number for the hospital. When a woman answered, I asked to speak with Kelli Jebat. I identified myself as Butch Wray.

"I'm sorry sir, who you wan` speak with?"

"Kelli Jebat, she's a nurse there."

"I'm sorry sir, she no longer work here. She gone."

"What? Are you sure? I thought I just saw, er, I mean..." I trailed off, not knowing what to say next.

"Yes, Miss Kelli's mother very sick, she go. She leave maybe one week ago."

"She left the island? Is she coming back?"

"No. She say she not come back. Mother very sick. Too bad, Miss Kelli very nice. Live here long time. Wha` was your name again, you friend of hers?"

"No...no, just someone that once knew her."

Back in my room I stood by the window and stared numbly down at the pier.

Good, one less complication to deal with.

Unless...she's with Wray and aboard the Gladiator.

I don't know how long I stood at the window but when I finally drifted back into focus I noticed the rain had stopped and sunshine was breaking through. It was going to be another hot, humid day. I decided to head for the pier.

I spent the rest of the day hanging around the dock and watching crews lazily working on their ships. One of the small freighters flew a British flag and as I walked closer to it I made out the name, *London Explorer.* I could see several men whom I assumed to be the crew, lounging around, smoking cigarettes and not doing much of anything. From the way they were dressed, or not dressed, I guessed their nationalities were mixed. Some were wearing shorts, flip-flops and nothing else; others wore greasy khakis with their shirttails hanging out. By the appearance of the boat, I assumed that none of them ever had a close relationship with a paint brush. As I walked by the thought occurred to me that I might have to be part of such a crew at some time, just to survive.

Later that night, back at the hotel bar, I nursed a couple of rum and cokes and ordered dinner to go. When I got back to my room, I didn't sit by the window this time. I just ate, showered, and went to bed trying very hard, for once, to not think about anything.

CHAPTER FORTY

The Gladiator

I slept late the next day and didn't even bother to look out the windows until mid-morning. When I did, I instinctively looked down at the apartment first. The only thing moving was the palm tree near the building. *Good, nothing to look at there anymore.* When I looked at the pier, it took a minute to register that something was different. *There was a new ship towards the end of the dock!*

After a quick shower, I grabbed my binoculars and was out the door fully awake. I didn't bother with anything to eat, I just headed straight to the pier. I hadn't really expected Wray and the *Gladiator* for another two days and I was aware that this new boat could be anybody, but still something told me this was the ship I had come so far to meet.

As I got closer to the dock I slowed my pace. If it was the *Gladiator*, I still had at least a day, maybe two, before Wray would be expecting me to show up. I wasn't sure whether Jimeen had told Wray what I looked like, but I figured it might be to my advantage to watch Wray from a distance for a couple of reasons. I might learn something about the man... and see what kind of company he keeps.

When I was about halfway down the pier, I could see the ship was tied up, bow out. Because of a low tide, the ship was partially hidden below the deck of the pier, but it looked like a typical rig boat with a high bridge deck and a long, low slung aft deck. It reminded me of the *Intrepid* and was probably close to two hundred feet long. I stopped and raised my binoculars. I could see a flag lying limp above the wheelhouse and as I focused in on it, a slight breeze blew and unfurled it. It was red, white and blue. The Stars and Stripes!

Lowering the glasses a little, I noticed a figure in the wheelhouse that appeared to be bent over working at a chart table. On the aft deck a couple of men were working on some equipment. I took a couple of steps closer and looked through my binoculars as an incoming swell lifted the fantail and exposed the name on the boat...*Gladiator.*

My heart started pounding and my hands were shaking. I was still far enough away from the boat that I felt no one on board would notice me, but I couldn't take another step closer. My hands were shaking so badly I couldn't focus the binoculars. For five or six minutes I stood there motionless letting my pulse slow down. When I looked again, the figure in the wheelhouse had disappeared.

I noticed a trash dumpster at the end of the dock and I picked up some scrap cardboard as if I were taking it to the dumpster. It would get me closer to the boat without anybody paying too much attention to me. I figured if Wray saw me looking at him, I'd just go aboard and introduce myself as the new engineer. Otherwise I'd make a slow pass along the far side of the dock and make mental notes of everything I could.

As I drew closer I could see the boat was in pretty good shape, at least a lot better than the *Intrepid*. She was painted red and white above the gunwales and had a dent-free black hull below. The long aft deck was clear of any tackle or gear, and looked like she could handle almost twice the load of the *Intrepid*. There were two standard life rafts, one on each side of the ship, mounted high on the boat deck just aft of the wheelhouse. A small crane arm and davits that could be used to raise and lower a small runabout or an inflatable, but I didn't see the Zodiac-type rig that I was hoping for.

Two big exhaust stacks framed the boat deck, and on the deck below I could see open hatches I assumed led to the engine room. As I reached the end of the dock I went behind the dumpster, tossed the cardboard into it, and then casually looked around the corner back at the boat. The wheelhouse was still empty, but on the bow I could see two Asian men applying a fresh coat of black paint to the anchor windlass. As I watched them, a man appeared in the wheelhouse and made motions as if he were talking on a VHF radio. Whoever it was remained in the shadows and kept the radio mike to his face, making it difficult to see his features. Slowly I lifted the binoculars and began to focus on the figure. I was a lot closer to the boat now and at first the image was extremely blurred; the man seemed to be putting the mike away…then suddenly the picture zapped into perfect focus. It was the same man's face that I had seen in Jimeen`s video. I was staring into the face of Butch Wray.

For a second I thought he was looking directly at me. I could see his mouth moving and he seemed to be agitated. Instinctively I jumped back behind the dumpster. When I peered around again, I saw Wray walk out from the bridge to the circular railing in front of the wheelhouse where he began barking orders at the two men below on the bow. I couldn't tell what he was saying, but from his hand movements and gestures, he didn't seem happy.

When I realized he hadn't seen me, my apprehension gave way to another emotion; deep hatred. I had an almost overwhelming urge to walk straight to the boat, get aboard and choke Wray to death with my bare hands. This was a man who hadn't given my brother's life, or mine, for that matter, a second thought. To Wray, people were disposable, trash that got in the way. He thought he was invincible. It was time to turn the tables.

I spent a few minutes behind the dumpster trying to calm down before I looked back at the boat. Wray was nowhere in sight. I gave it a couple more minutes then started back down the dock. Just as I was about to pass abeam of the *Gladiator*, a sea bag came flying up from below and landed on the dock about ten yards ahead of me. A moment later a man's head appeared and stopped on the ladder that extended up from the boat. The man flipped another smaller bag over his shoulder onto the dock before climbing the rest of the way up and onto the pier. He was well over six feet tall with a full beard and belly, and looked to be German or Scandinavian. He was muttering to himself in a language I couldn't understand, but I assumed from his manner, he was pissed about something. Once on the dock, he quickly hefted his sea bag over his shoulder, grabbed his other bag, and started down the pier.

I slowed my pace so I could follow a few yards behind him. Once the man reached the end of the pier, he stopped and set his bag down. He took a bandana out and wiped his face. He seemed to be trying to figure out which way to go from there. A couple of locals walked by and he stopped them. After a short exchange, they both turned and pointed towards town and the sailor headed off in that direction. He didn't go far before he found what he was looking for, an open-air bar on a corner in town.

I walked in behind him as he dragged a steel wire chair, screeching across the concrete floor to a table in the corner. He threw down his sea bag, ran his hand through his curly blond hair, and sat down with a thump. There were no other customers in the place.

I walked past him and pretended to look at a menu that was scrawled on a chalk board behind a bored-looking bartender. With great indifference, the bartender got up and brushed past me to take the sailor's order. I heard the man order two Heinekens. When the bartender came back, I ordered a Heineken as well, making sure I said it loud enough for the sailor to hear.

The bartender opened a glass cooler, pulled three bottles out, then came back and set one in front of me and took the others to the man. The sailor had already thrown one of the beers down by the time I sauntered over to him and offered a toast to the makers of such a fine brew.

"Yah, eesh fine beer" he said as he raised his glass, draining the second one.

"You got time for another?" I asked him. "I'd like to talk to you about something."

He gazed up at me with a quizzical look, then burped, wiped foam from his mouth and gestured for me to sit.

I scrambled for something innocuous to say as I sat down. "Ah…you know these waters very well? I'm…ah...I'm an engineer and I've been hired to take a boat back to the U.S …"

He looked at me for a long time before he answered, then he laughed. "Do I know deez vaters? Ha! I`ve zailed da whole vorld!" Then he stuck out a hand that looked more like a scarred-up ham and said, "I am Brock."

"Jack Tatcher," I said as my hand disappeared in his.

"Vell Jacque Taucher, vut you vant to know?"

"Well I, a... thought I saw you get off the *Gladiator*. She came in from Singapore, didn't she?"

"Ya she did, and ya I vus on da damn ship. Vy?

Brock's demeanor suddenly dropped a notch.

"Oh, a friend of mine is working her way over from Singapore. I just wondered if she might be aboard."

"A voman? On dey *Gladiator*?" He looked at me like I had two heads. "No, vimen are bad luck on ships. I haf bad luck enough vith da captain. I am so glad to be off dat ship. Ach, he vas terrible! Neva vill I zail wit dat man again! He ez inzane!"

"Hard to get along with, I take it?"

"Ya, crazy! Alvays sneaking around da boat. He trust no vone. He vas paranoid man. Cameras hevey vare!"

"Cameras?"

"Ya, cameras on top of da veelhouse, in da engine vroom, cameras on da vantail."

I knew it wasn't unusual for a ship to have cameras mounted in the engine room in case of fire or cameras mounted on deck to help with blind spots when maneuvering the ship, but Wray seemed to have an inordinate amount of cameras around the boat. I remembered what Jimeen had said, *'he has a thing about cameras.'*

I ordered more oil from the bartender and let my new friend rattle on. According to Brock, there were four cameras mounted atop the wheelhouse, two port, two starboard and were aimed fore and aft. There was a camera in the engine room and two others in the passageways below deck and one on the fantail. These areas could all be monitored from two small screens on the control consul in the wheelhouse.

"Da crazee focker say da cameras are for da pirates, but I know bedder, dey are for spying on da crew! I vouldn`t doubt he put cameras in da head so to catch us playing vith ourselves!"

Brock belly-laughed his way into a coughing spell, which he finally quelled with a couple of swigs of beer. Once he straightened out and fluffed up his beard he started in again.

"Vone time I go by da captain`s vroom and I see him putting a pistal under heez bunk. Da man vent nutso jelling at me, saying I vas sneaking up on him! Ha! Me! I ask you, you tink I could sneak up on sum von?"

I looked at his size. He had a good point. With all the cameras aboard, I knew it was going to be hard for me to dispose of Wray and not get caught on tape. I would have to remember to destroy a camera or two if I had time.

It was Wray`s face on camera that brought me here, but the only air time I wanted for him now would be the time he spent in the air from the upper deck of the *Gladiator* to the sea.

CHAPTER FORTY-ONE

"Hello the boat," I yelled down from the pier. I was standing near a ladder that led down to the aft deck of the *Gladiator* but I didn't see any of the crew. I was just about to yell again when one of the guys I'd seen the day before, poked his bare, shaved head out of the port engine room hatch. He looked up at me and shaded his eyes. I could see he had a round, clean-shaven face, but from this distance, I couldn't tell if he was squinting or smiling.

"Good morning. Is Captain Wray aboard?"

He said something that sounded like "yes," then stepped the rest of the way out of the hatch and waved me aboard. I backed my way down the ladder, balancing my sea bag on my shoulder, and turned to greet the man. "Hi, I'm…Jack Tatcher."

"I am Kim," he said, with a short bow. Up close I could see he could have been the poster boy for the "happy face" caricature. He had a perpetual smile and dancing eyes. As I returned his bow, I felt, more then saw, a figure appear off to the side and above me on the boat deck. I turned and looked up at him. It was my turn to shade my eyes from the sun, but I could tell it was Wray. My voice almost cracked, but I got it out: "Captain?"

Instead of answering, he looked at the man standing next to me. "Kim, bring him up here, bring him to the wheelhouse."

Kim bent to pick up my bag when Wray bellowed down, "He can carry his own bag!"

Kim's eyes met mine briefly, then he nodded his head for me to follow him. We stepped through an open hatch that led through a crew's lounge and on to the galley. Just forward of the crew's lounge we started up a ladder to the wheelhouse. The configuration of the interior deck space was almost identical to the layout of the *Intrepid*. At the base of a ladder, I sat my bag down and followed Kim up to meet Wray.

When we entered the wheelhouse, Wray had his back to us looking at a chart. He let us stand there and squirm for more than a few seconds, but finally, he turned around and I was face to face with my brother's killer.

Time seemed to stand still as we sized each other up. He was shorter than I expected but his facial features were exactly what had burned into my brain ever since I saw his face on the film from Jimeen's camera. But now that I was three feet away from him I could see his dark beady eyes. I noticed a slight nervous twitch in his jaw. His black hair had a greasy sheen to it and he looked like he hadn't shaved in a day or two. It took everything I had to force a smile and extend my hand.

"Hi, I'm Jack Tatcher."

Our eyes locked for a minute. I figured he could see right through me. Finally he shook my hand and said, "You're the engineer the old man sent, right?"

"Yep, that's me."

"Okay, let's go. I'll show you where you bunk."

Kim stayed behind while I followed Wray back down the ladder. I picked up my sea bag, then followed Wray down another ladder to the deck below. We took a few steps down a narrow passageway stopping in front of an open door.

"Here's where you'll sleep," Wray said as he gestured for me to enter the room. The cabin was tiny and cramped with one bunk bed and one small closet. I didn't care. It wasn't going to be home for long.

"Now," Wray said in an officious voice, "empty everything out of your sea bag. Lay everything on the bunk."

It caught me by surprise and when I hesitated, he stared at me and said, "It's my policy to know exactly what's brought aboard this ship. Especially people I've never met before. On the bunk."

I did what he asked without a word. When I was through, I stepped back and let him examine everything. While he was going through my things, Brock's words echoed through my brain. I understood why Brock had said the things he did, this guy *was* paranoid, but then again, he had good reason to be.

When Wray finished he said, "Very good. Now while you're putting your things away, I'll send Kim to show you around the boat and the engine room. Remember, Kim and two other crew members were hired to help bring this boat from Singapore and nothing else. One guy has already left the ship so we won't worry about him. Kim you've already met and there's another guy around here somewhere named Peng, or Pong, or some gook name like that. Anyway, they'll be getting off the boat as soon as the rest of the crew get here. As far as you're concerned, you've been hired as the engineer to take this boat back to the U.S. That's all you know, and that's all you need to know, got it?"

I resisted the urge to slam him against the wall and take care of business right then and there. Instead I shrugged and said, "Yeah, no problem."

I spent two hours with Kim who showed me everything he could think of on the boat. At first he seemed jumpy and would look around nervously while explaining something, but after awhile, he seemed to relax a little. He really did know the boat well and he seemed to appreciate some of the questions I asked him, especially when we were in the engine room. At one point, I mentioned the cameras around the boat. He looked down at his feet before answering, "Yes, for safety." Then he looked me square in the eye and said, "You be careful. You be careful what you do."

As we were climbing back up from the engine room, I asked Kim, "Where's the rest of the crew? Isn't there another man aboard?"

"Yes, his name is Peng." Kim kept walking along the aft deck then looked over the rail and waved at me to look over the side. Six feet below us, standing in an inflatable, a Zodiac, was the man I saw working with Kim the day before. He had a paint roller in his hand and was intensely applying a coat of paint to the hull. His head was shaved as well but was dotted with black paint. Kim said something in his language, and the man looked up and smiled without missing a stroke. I smiled back…we did have a Zodiac!

I still had a half smile on my face when we caught up with Wray in the crew's lounge. He was sitting at the settee with a cup of coffee. He caught my smile as I stepped through the hatch so I tried pawning it off as being happy with what Kim had shown me and said, "I'm glad to see Detroit's in the engine room. They're reliable, easy to work on."

"Well you shouldn't have to work on them," Wray growled. "They were just overhauled…in fact, I don't want you touching `em unless you check with me first." Wray then turned to Kim who was just about to pour himself a cup of coffee. "Kim, go help what`s-his-name finish up, then put the Zodiac away. I'd like to go over a few things with, a…Jack."

Kim set down the cup, turned and headed back out the way he'd come. I picked up Kim's cup and poured myself some coffee. Then I sat down opposite Wray. When he was satisfied Kim was out of earshot he leaned in closely."OK, here's the deal. I don't know what the old man has told you or what you got going with him, and I don't give a shit, that's your business. What I expect out of you is this: once we're out to sea, you keep the engines running and stand wheel watches, and that's basically it. One crew member is already here in town and the other I expect in two days. I wanna leave right after they get on board. It's extremely important that we keep to this schedule. Tomorrow morning we'll fuel up. Kim and the other guy have fueled this boat before so they can take care of handling the lines. I want you to stay with them and keep sounding the tanks as we go along, I don't want one ounce of fuel oil spilled, not that I give a shit about this dirty fuckin` harbor, I just don't want any attention drawn to this boat in any way. You with me?"

Wray`s jaw twitched as he waited for a reaction from me. When I nodded, he continued. "Okay, the fueling should take about four hours. After that I've arranged for fresh fruits and vegetables to be delivered. We can top off our fresh water supply at the same time. Then tomorrow, I want to move the boat over to the shipyard first thing in the morning. Shipyard personnel will load some oil drilling equipment on the aft deck. I don't want you touchin` any of it; they'll secure everything. Once we set out, I want to be in San Francisco in thirty days. In the meantime, until we leave, I expect you to stay aboard and get to know the boat and engine room inside and out. I don't want any screw-ups. You with me?"

I heard myself answer, "I'm with you."

"Good, any questions?"

I lowered my voice slightly and asked, "By the way, which way we goin` home, you know, north or south end of the Philippines?"

"Why does that concern you?"

I shrugged, trying to stay cool. "I just thought if we go the southern route we'll probably burn more fuel. I just want to know if we can top this boat off and still handle the load, that's all."

"Don't worry about that. We won't be affected by the weight of our cargo. I can tell you we'll be going around the Philippines to the south, which does mean bucking some currents and using more fuel that way, but there's less pirate activity that route. Besides, we've got plenty of range. When we fuel, I want these tanks topped off. Got it?"

"Sounds good to me," I said and tried not to smile. It did sound good to me. Things were shaping up nicely, not only was there a Zodiac for my escape, but we were also taking a route through the southern chain of the Philippine Islands, putting us very close to land for at least twenty-four hours. It was all the window I should need.

"Okay, there are some log books and schematics in the engine room. I suggest you study `em. When we leave here, you should know the fuel and ballast systems blindfolded."

As far as I was concerned it wouldn't be a problem. And I didn't really care how much fuel we were taking on, just as long as we had enough to get to the Philippines, after all, I didn't plan on being around when the *Gladiator* reached San Francisco.

Wray got up and took his coffee cup to the sink in the galley. "Right now, I've gotta get over to the shipyard. I wanna make sure these slant-eyed fucks can get a fuel barge over to us first thing tomorrow morning."

As he climbed up the ladder to the dock, I thought about the concern I'd had ever since I decided to come after Wray. *Could I actually kill this man?* I still wasn't 100 percent positive I could, but every time he opened his mouth he sure made a case for it.

CHAPTER FORTY-TWO

The next morning as Kim, Peng and I were having breakfast, a small tugboat gently nosed a fuel barge alongside. Before I could even set my coffee down, Wray came bellowing into the galley. "Alright, you guys get going, the barge is here. You can eat later."

As Peng and Kim headed out the hatch, Wray pulled me aside and said, "Remember what I said about a fuel spill. I don't think these dumb fucks even have a coast guard or anything like that, but just in case, I don't want to give some asshole a reason to be snooping around here if we don't have to."

The man certainly had a way with words.

Fortunately, Wray stayed out of the way, the fueling process went smoothly and we didn't spill a drop. It even felt good, sweating and working alongside Kim and Peng as if I were a legitimate sailor preparing to get a ship underway. As we were dragging the fuel hoses back to the barge, a produce truck that had been parked by the *London Explorer* made its way down to us. We quickly formed a chain gang and for the next hour passed down fruits and vegetables until we had it all stowed. Finally, with the empty cardboard containers piled high on the aft deck we sat down for a break.

It didn't last long. Wray walked out from the wheelhouse and stood on the boat deck above us. "Hey, Kim, get that fuckin` cardboard off this boat! You know maggots and worms love to nest in that crap. Get rid of it, now!"

As he turned back into the wheelhouse, he said over his shoulder, "I better not find any of those crawly fuckers in my cereal!"

We rousted ourselves up immediately and started hauling the trash up to the bin on the dock. As we were throwing it in the dumpster, a sailor from the *London Explorer* made his way down the dock dragging some cardboard of his own.

"Ello mate," he said to me as he tossed his trash.

"Howdy," I said, feeling very much the Yank that I was. "Looks like you guys are gettin` ready to sail."

"Oh yeah, I think we be leavin` soon`s the rest of the crew gets back from town and gets their bloody shots."

"Shots"? Something in the back of my brain twitched.

"Yeah some bloke in a white smock came down the dock, said we`d been exposed to something. Said `eh needed to come aboard to give us all a shot. We told him half the crew was in town for the evenin`, likely havin` a pint or two. That tightened his cheeks abit, so `eh says `eel be back tomorrow afternoon. Said the port captain won't let us sail till `eh gives us our inoculations."

I wasn't sure if I was having a deju vu moment, but what he said next jolted me. "The lil faggot thought `eh was a big shot, you know, like a doctor or something, but I know he was only a nurse. The bloody hell, I say, but what can you do?" The sailor gave me a half salute and turned to leave.

Only a nurse.

"Wait," I stammered. "You're...you're leaving…now? Right away?"

"Well we weren't due to leave for a couple of days but ah`m thinking we be leavin` soon`s we can. No sense sittin` round `ere in quarantine."

"Ah…back to England?"

"No, we be headed your way, to the States that is."

"Empty?" I asked. I had noticed that there wasn't any cargo on the *Explorer's* decks.

He suddenly acted as if he'd already said too much. "Well, ah thinks one of the oil companies in the U.S. wants to refit her, or something like that. Listen mate…a …smooth sailin` to you now. I gotta get me arse back."

I stood there numbly as I watched him walk quickly toward his ship.

Slowly the gears in my pea brain began to mesh. The light bulb was growing brighter. Now things made more sense. It had to have been that little asshole that came aboard the *Intrepid* the day we left port that planted the transmitter! The same guy that manhandled Kelli as we were leaving.

But now what? Can I be sure that Kelli wasn't somehow mixed up in any of this? Does this change my plans at all?

I shuddered as one of my questions was answered almost immediately. "Hey!" Wray yelled from outside the wheelhouse, "There's still lots of shit on deck down here. I said I want this crap off my boat, NOW!!"

I almost thanked him under my breath as Kim and I headed back down the ladder. *No, there won't be any change in my immediate plans.*

The countdown had begun.

CHAPTER FORTY-THREE

The next morning on Wray's order, I fired up the main engines and made ready for the short run across the harbor. Kim and Peng took care of handling the lines on deck and within minutes, we eased away from the dock. Ten minutes later we idled up to the shipyard pier. We positioned ourselves adjacent to a crane where some drill casings, ship's propellers and generators had been set on the dock. Wray made it a point to remind us that we wouldn't have to touch anything; that the shipyard boys would handle everything, including securing the equipment to the deck of the *Gladiator*. That was more than fine with me. It gave me a chance to get a close-up look at how the Zodiac was set up.

When I was sure Wray was watching the loading process, I made my way up to the boat deck which was behind the bridge and eight feet above the main deck. I noticed two cameras and spotlights mounted port and starboard on top of the wheelhouse as Brock had mentioned. Both cameras and lights were pointed aft, and down each side of the boat. From the way the cameras were angled, it didn't appear that the Zodiac would be in view.

I wanted to know exactly what kind of shape the inflatable was in, if there was gasoline aboard, and what I would need to do to launch it. I noticed that the craft was positioned just below a small hydraulic boom and rigged in a way that would make it very easy for one man to lower the boat to the water. I wouldn't even have to slow the ship to make my getaway. I could just lower the inflatable until the stern was dragging in the water, crawl over the gunwale and get in. The natural roll of the ship would allow me to release the hook.

I pulled back the tarp that was covering the small boat and saw the oars strapped in place. I could see a hose from a five gallon gas can was still attached to the outboard motor. I leaned over and lifted the gas can. It was heavy.

Three hours later, half the aft deck was covered with equipment, mostly forty-foot lengths of drill pipe running fore and aft. As the crane operator picked up the last piece of pipe from the dock, Wray barked at me to start the main engines, and Kim and Peng made ready to cast off. As we slowly made our way back to the main pier, I joined Wray in the wheelhouse. "Well, I guess we're ready to get underway then, huh Skip?" The fact that I used a term of informal respect like "skip" for Wray almost stuck in my throat, but I was feeling pretty confident after checking out the situation with the Zodiac.

"Yeah, soon as the other guys get here. One guy's bringing some spare parts for the fuel separator that the old man is sending along. You can't trust the fuel oil these fucks give you in this part of the world and I don't want to take a chance on the centrifuge goin' tits up half way across the Pacific."

"Yeah, I know what you mean," I said truthfully, remembering the episode on the *Intrepid*. I was trying to draw Wray into a conversation, trying to find out if he knew Kelli.

"So, you goin' ashore tonight?" I asked. "You know, last night in town and all."

"Hell no, I'm not going ashore," he practically screamed. "And neither are you. Nobody's gonna screw this trip up! You with me?"

I could tell I was pressing my luck, the veins in Wray's neck were already bulging, but I kept on, like we were becoming buddies. "Yeah, sure Skip. I just heard there were some nice looking women in town, thought you might want to ...you know, get laid or something."

I tried to make the last part sound funny, like I was kidding, but it struck a nerve with him. "Get laid!!??" He sneered. "Screw one of these fuckin' gooks? I wouldn't screw one of these sluts with *your* dick!"

"You don't like the women around here?"

"As a matter of fact I don't, but what I really don't like is you asking all these stupid fuckin' questions." Then he turned to look at me. "You with me?" His habit of saying, *You with me?* was really getting irritating.

"Yeah, yeah, okay." I made a point of yawning and stretching like it was no big deal. "Well, I guess I'll go help Kim and Peng get ready to tie up."

Wray said nothing as I left the wheelhouse.

That night, as Kim and Peng were cleaning up after the evening meal, Wray went over the plan for the next day. "The guy the old man is sending us should be coming in on the afternoon flight tomorrow. Kim and Peng will be flying out at the same time. The other crew member is already in town and, well, I guess he'll come aboard tomorrow too."

Wray sighed a little when he mentioned the *other* crew member, almost like he wasn't too happy about it."There's just one more thing we may have to wait on, but it's none of your business and shouldn't delay us long in any case. We should be sailing on the morning tide, day after tomorrow."

He paused for a second then looked me in the eye. "You comfortable with the engine room layout? The systems, air compressors, lube oil? Think you could find everything in the dark if you had to?"

"Yeah, sure, I'm fine. I'm ready to go."

"Good," Wray said as he took his coffee cup to the sink for Peng to wash. "I don't like surprises."

The next morning my thoughts returned to the *London Explorer*. I was almost sure now they were smugglers and were probably being set up just as we had been on the *Intrepid*. I assumed it was Wray who was orchestrating the set-up but I didn't know why. *Was there another boat with a bigger load out there?* Part of me wanted to warn the *Explorer*, another side of me said to let it go. For all I knew, the crew of the *Explorer* could be a bunch of bad guys, ala Butch Wray. Besides, if I said anything to the crew on the *Explorer*, I'd almost certainly jeopardize my situation. I decided to let it go for the time being.

In the short time that I'd been aboard the *Gladiator*, I'd developed a respect for Kim and Peng. They were friendly to me, hardworking and seemingly honest. I would be sorry to see them go. Later that day when the time came for them to leave, I offered to help carry their gear to the end of the dock. Surprisingly, Wray didn't object other than to say, "Don't be goin' into town and havin' a beer with them or anything. We got shit to do here. Besides, the other crew could show up anytime now and as soon as they do, I wanna have a little pow-wow with everybody at the same time, you with me?"

"Yeah, I'm with you," I mumbled.

Kim, Peng and I walked to the end of the pier where I sat down the small bag I was carrying and turned to the men to say goodbye.

"You watch out Mr. Jack, that captain is a bad man, okay?" Kim said.

I really wanted to tell them what I had in store for Wray, I'm sure they would have approved. "Yes, I know he is Kim. He's a very bad man, but I'll be okay," then added with a wink, "cause I might just be a bad man too."

That evening it was just me and Wray aboard the ship. I thought about killing him every time he turned his back to me. I knew with two other crewmen coming aboard, this might be my best chance to do it. I also knew if I killed him and then and took off, I would definitely be the number one suspect in his murder. If I waited until we were out to sea, his disappearance might be reported a little differently, if it was reported at all. I told myself to be patient, the right time would come. Tomorrow I'd meet the other crew and Wray will assign us our watch schedule. Soon we'll be at sea and Wray`s time on earth will just about be over.

CHAPTER FORTY-FOUR

The first shock came mid-morning just as I was coming up the ladder out of the engine room. I was a couple of steps away from the hatch that opened to the aft deck when I heard a voice coming from the deck that froze me. "Okay, everything's in place." Something about the voice sounded vaguely familiar. Then I heard Wray's voice. "I still don't know why you're doing this. You'll probably just get seasick and not be worth a fuck to anybody. If I didn't know better, I'd think you didn't trust me!"

The first voice had a trace of a foreign accent. "Well let's just say I'd like to be around when the money comes down for this one. Besides, I've got sea time under my belt, you more than anyone should know that."

"Yeah but whadda``bout your job? Whadda they gonna think? You can't just leave!"

"Look, we've been over this, I told you, I gave them notice two weeks ago, besides..."

Suddenly an air compressor in the engine room kicked on, making me jump just enough that I made a noise of my own. Afraid that Wray and whoever he was talking to may have heard me, I started whistling and rattling the handrail, making as much noise as I could before stepping out onto the deck, pretending to be oblivious. When I did step out of the hatch and turned around, I certainly didn't need to pretend I was startled. The vaguely familiar voice belonged to the weasel from the hospital…the *nurse*!

"Oh, hi," I muttered, trying to act surprised, yet nonchalant at the same time.

Wray seemed annoyed that I suddenly popped into the picture. My heart was pounding, waiting for the sleazeball to say, "Hey, I know you from somewhere don't I?" Instead, he gave no indication that we'd met. He simply studied me and waited for Wray to say something. Wray was still glaring at me as he cleared his throat and introduced us."Ah, this is Rik Craven. He'll be sailing with us. Rik, this is our engineer, Jack…a …"

"Tatcher," I finished for him and extended my hand to Craven. His handshake was limp and clammy. I gave him a closer look. He had a wispy mustache that he may have been trying to grow for months. I did remember his Asian features, black piercing eyes and short cropped hair. We exchanged hellos and then I said, "Well, I better finish checking the fuel oil vents." I started toward the bow with my heart pounding. I stopped at the nearest fuel vent, a goose-neck affair that rose about six feet up from the deck near the base of the wheelhouse. As I pretended to inspect it, I stole a look back at Wray and Craven. They were still standing in the same spot and looking my way. I moved on to the next vent and went through the same pantomime. When I looked back again, they had moved off among the equipment on deck and had resumed their conversation.

It took awhile, but my heart rate finally slowed to a somewhat normal pace. I told myself that nothing had changed. I would just have to be extra careful. I would have to stay away from Craven as much as possible. I reminded myself that the only person in the world that had any idea why I was aboard the *Gladiator* was a world away, and he would be rooting for me to accomplish my goal.

After awhile I gathered myself and headed below to my bunk. I needed to digest the situation. The thought of staying away from Craven was short lived. When I opened the door to the cabin, I found Craven sitting on my bunk.

"Oh, hi. Looks like we're bunking together," he said. "I hope you don't mind."

My gaze didn't waver. "No, that's fine."

"Excuse me for saying so, but you don't look like it's fine."

"No, I just thought, well…I thought you'd be bunking a little closer to the captain, you know. Those cabins topside are a little more spacious, that's all."

Craven gave a short laugh, "Well, for one thing, I don't think the captain is overjoyed with me being aboard, but that's his problem." He paused. "Ah, say …it's Jack right? Jack, look there's something I'd like to ask you."

I just looked at him and waited.

"I've got a bad back. Would you mind if I took the bottom bunk?"

Relief surged through me for about a second, but was quickly replaced with anger. *Yeah, I do mind, you little shit. And I minded when you planted your little device aboard the Intrepid, and I minded when you grabbed Kelli. And I mind that you're even on this boat!*

"Yeah, I...uh...I know how it is with a bad back. Help yourself."

I quickly tossed my pillow to the upper bunk and headed topside. I needed some air fast. I took a lap around the aft deck, ducking under some of the drill pipe as I went along. As I made my way up the starboard side, my nerves began to calm. I slowed when I neared the Zodiac. *It won't be long now. Just stay cool and I'll be in that dingy and off this boat… and on the run.*

Later that evening, I had a very frosty dinner with Wray and Craven. The fourth crewman hadn't shown up yet and Wray was reluctant to talk about any further plans until the man was on board. Craven offered nothing in the way of conversation, which was fine with me. As soon as I could, I headed off to the engine room to go over some things. I wanted to make sure I could keep the boat running for at least a couple of days, and I also wanted to stay away from Craven and Wray. I was beginning to feel like the engine room might be the only safe haven for me.

CHAPTER FORTY-FIVE

I was in the engine room when Wray yelled down from the aft deck."Hey Chief! Come on up here. The spare parts for the centrifuge just came aboard."

If the parts were here, that meant that the last crew member had arrived. With some anxiety, I headed up the ladder. When I stepped out onto the deck my heart almost stopped. In the fading light I saw a man standing next to Wray. He looked a little different in blue jeans and a khaki shirt, but there was still enough light to see who it was. It was the old man.

"Hello Jack. I see you found your way here," Alan Jimeen said as he walked towards me.

Bewildered, I stumbled, "Ah, yeah, no problem...ah, what are you doin' here?" I couldn't hide my shock. Before Jimeen could answer, Wray said, "That's a damn good question, ain't it Al?" Again, Wray didn't look too happy with the turn of events.

"Yeah, well, like I was telling Butch here, I had to make a last minute change in personnel. The other guy couldn't make it, so I'm taking his place. I really couldn't trust anybody else, so, I'm sailing with you guys."

I looked straight into his eyes for a hint of what was going on, but I couldn't read anything. "I'll tell you more in a minute," he said as he kicked the box at his feet. "But hey, I brought you these parts for your fuel-oil separator. You want 'em in the engine room?"

Wray stepped between us and said, "Yeah, he wants 'em in the engine room and he can take them there himself. Right now Al, I wanna talk to you. You'll share my cabin. Bring your bag and come with me. Tatcher, give us twenty minutes and then meet us in the galley."

I muttered "Okay," as I picked up the box before anybody could tell how badly I had begun to shake. As soon as I made it below, I took a few deep breathes and stowed the box of parts under a shelf by the control board. I stood there, not moving, not knowing what to do next. Then I remembered the cameras. *Were they on now?* I straightened up, grabbed a rag and began wiping down some imaginary oil leaks on the port engine. I even went through the motion of trying to whistle, but as dry as my mouth was, I couldn't make a sound. For the next twenty minutes I tried to figure out my next move. *Was Jimeen here to help me? He did call me Jack instead of Sonny, didn't he? Has he changed his mind? Or is he up there now telling Wray who I am? What the hell was going on?*

I thought about making a break for it. I could make it to the ladder and then to the dock and just take off. But I'd need clothes, my passport and money, and they were all in my cabin and I'd have to go through the galley to get there. I was almost frantic trying to sort things out. Then I thought about Tim and an almost calming sensation came over me. I was here to do a job. I'd come too far to panic now. I visualized Wray hitting the water after falling from the top deck of the *Gladiator.* Soon my pulse slowed down and I stopped shaking. I took a deep breath and started up the ladder toward the galley.

Just outside the hatch to the galley, I noticed a Crescent wrench lying on the deck. It wouldn't be as good as a gun, but then I was never very good with those anyway. I picked up the wrench and put it in my back pocket.

Wray, Craven and Jimeen were all seated around the table just off the galley. They all looked up as I came through the hatch. None of them were smiling.

"Sit down," Wray snapped.

As I sat down on the bench seat, I slipped the wrench out of my pocket and tucked in under my right leg.

"Okay, we're all here," Wray began. "Not exactly who I thought would be my crew, but I don't have time to fuck around anymore." Wray looked at Jimeen briefly then continued.

"I don't like surprises as some of you know, and if it weren't for the fact that things are in motion now, I'd be tempted to call this whole thing off. But I've got too much invested now and timing is crucial, so here's the deal: we're leaving the first thing in the morning. Now, I know everyone here has experience standing wheel watches, but just to make sure we're all on the same page, I want everyone on the bridge right after we cast off. I want to make sure everybody can read the radar and steer this fucking boat if they have to. As soon we make open water, I'll set our course and speed and punch in the autopilot. And once I do that, I don't want anybody touching anything."

Wray's jaw twitched as he took a moment to look each one of us in the eye to make sure he was getting his message across.

"No throttle changes, no course changes, no nothin' less it's an emergency, and then it better damn well be one. If you got any questions about anything while you're on watch, remember, my cabin is just below the bridge and I can be at the helm within seconds. We'll stand three hour watches with Rik taking six-to-nine. Tatcher, you'll take the nine-to-twelve and I'll relieve you and take the mid watch till three. Al, you'll relieve me and stand the three-to-six." And then, like the proverbial fingernails across a chalk board he asked, "You with me?"

From the minute I had entered the galley, I'd been stealing glances at Jimeen, trying to get some kind of signal, but every time I caught his eye, he looked away. But since Wray had included me on the watch schedule, I could only assume Jimeen hadn't tipped him off about me…so far.

Wray stood up and poured himself a cup of coffee, "I wanna be within four hundred miles of San Francisco in three weeks. We need to be there no later than the 28th." Wray paused and looked at Craven. "Right, Rik? Isn't that what you figure?"

"Yeah, that should time out right."

"Okay, Wray continued. "I want everybody up by five o'clock tomorrow morning. Tatcher, the first thing you do is warm up the engines. The rest of you will secure anything that isn't battened down. I wanna shove off by six. Any questions?" When we had none, Wray said, "Okay, Al, there's a few more things I wanna talk to you about." With a nod towards Craven and me, Wray dismissed us by saying, "And you two, I suggest you turn in and get some sleep."

As I got up to leave, I scrambled to think of some way to get next to Jimeen, I had to find out what he was doing here. I took a couple of steps and threw out a hint. "Well, I've got a few things I wanna sort out in the engine room yet, I…. I think I'll putter around down there for awhile."

"You'll have three weeks to sort things out." Wray said. "Go to your quarters."

This time it wasn't a suggestion.

Reluctantly I turned to go below. Just as I was leaving the galley Jimeen called out, "Hey, son."

I froze for an instant before I turned around.

"You forget this?"

He was holding the Crescent wrench in his hand.

During the night I half expected Jimeen to knock on my door. If he was going to tell me something, he better do it before six in the morning. But with Craven in the room, that presented a problem. Several times I got up to use the head and browsed around the galley, ostensibly to get a snack or something to drink, hoping Jimeen would do the same. I knew that once we cast off the lines, there were no stopping points between where we were and the U.S. and I sure as hell wasn't going to take the chance of sneaking back into the States aboard the *Gladiator*.

Finally, I gave up on Jimeen and went back to my bunk. Maybe in the morning while I was warming up the engines, Jimeen would let me know what the hell was going on. In the meantime, I slept fitfully, listening to Craven snore.

CHAPTER FORTY-SIX

Departure

Wray and Jimeen were already in the galley with cups of coffee in their hands when I joined them at 5:15 the next morning. Jimeen nodded causally. Wray just looked at me and growled, "Go get those engines warmed up, now."

I quickly turned and headed out the hatch before I lost control of myself.

Fifteen minutes later, everything was ready in the engine room but I still hadn't talked with Jimeen. If he was here to try and stop me from killing Wray, I had to know. There was still time for me to step off the boat. I gave it another five minutes and then headed topside. One way or another, I was going to talk to the man.

When I stepped out of the engine room hatch, I could see Wray standing outside of the wheelhouse, looking down at Craven who was manning the forward cleat. Jimeen was on the aft cleat waiting for Wray's command to cast off. A couple of sailors from another boat stood by on the dock. As I made my way over to Jimeen I heard Wray yell down at me, "Tatcher! You ready to go?" I ignored him and kept walking toward Jimeen. When I was close enough, I asked him, "Are you going to try to stop me from killing this prick?"

Jimeen just shook his head and said, "No."

Wray yelled again. "Hey! Tatcher! You ready to go?" Again I ignored him and looked straight into Jimeen's eyes. "Are you going to help me?"

Jimeen studied me for a moment and then gave me the same response as before,"No."

"Goddamnit Jack, I'm talking to you! Are you ready or not?"

Slowly I turned around, looked up at Wray, and smiled. "Yeah, I am. Are you?"

"Wha...?All right goddammit, let's go!" Wray threw up his hands to the sailors on the dock indicating it was time to throw off the lines and cast off. Seconds later the diesels rumbled and the *Gladiator* slowly began to separate from the dock. The die was cast. We were on our way.

An hour later we all met in the wheelhouse for our briefing. Wray laid out the sea rules again and was anal about several things, including how he wanted us to dispose of garbage.

"Any trash that goes overboard I want tied off in a plastic bag with holes poked into it so it'll sink. I don't want to leave a trail that might wash ashore. You with me?"

I couldn't help but wonder if Wray's body might wash ashore. I assumed that sharks would get him first, unless of course, they didn't eat their own.

After our meeting on the bridge, Craven took the first wheel watch with Wray standing close by. Jimeen and I went out on deck and made our way forward to the anchor windlass. As we watched the island of Labuan grow smaller on the horizon I said, "Well, no turning back now, huh?"

"No, no there isn't," Jimeen answered in a wistful voice.

"So....you gonna tell me what the hell you're doing here?"

"To tell you the truth, I'm not too sure myself."

"But you're not here to tip Wray off? You're not going to interfere with my plan?"

"No, you do what you have to."

"By myself?"

"By yourself."

There were a few moments of silence, and then just before he walked off, Jimeen looked at me and said, "By the way, I don't think it's a good idea if you and I appear too chummy."

I watched him walk away and wondered what was going on with him. I decided the only thing I could do was take him for his word that he wouldn't interfere with my plan. I needed to concentrate on Wray.

For a moment I thought that maybe killing Wray was too good for him. I wanted him to suffer. I thought about him in the water surrounded by sharks. I thought about how Tim suffered the last days of his life and I wanted Wray to suffer as well. I was hoping he would still be conscious when the first shark tore into his flesh. I toyed with the idea of telling him who I was just before I tossed him overboard. I wanted to see fear in his eyes. I wanted him to know why he was about to die.

Wray didn't know it, but when he made out the watch list he played right into my hands. He would be relieving me from my watch at midnight, which would mean that Craven and Jimeen would most likely be asleep when I killed Wray. If my luck held, neither Craven nor Jimeen would have a reason to wander up to the bridge for two or three hours. I should be long gone by then.

I realized that when the time came to toss Wray, we could be twenty or thirty miles from any of the Philippine Islands, but I guessed that the Zodiac had at least two hours of fuel aboard, which should be enough for me to reach shore. And hopefully, I'd have time to set the autopilot to steer the *Gladiator* towards open ocean. I didn't really care if the ship ended up on the rocks along with Craven, but I didn't want to see anybody else get hurt. And for some reason, I did care about Jimeen. He seemed a little out of place in the drug world, and although he had been cool towards me every since he came aboard the *Gladiator,* I felt that maybe in a different time and place, we might even be friends. Then I reminded myself that in a few days, I would never see him again.

I was a little apprehensive about standing my first morning watch at 9 a.m. I thought Wray would be looking over my shoulder to make sure I could be trusted to stand the later night watch. As it turned out, Wray spent more time plotting our course and muttering to himself, then he did critiquing my helm technique.

Later that afternoon, I was just about to step through the engine room hatch when I saw Jimeen emerging from the equipment on the aft deck. “Hey, Al, what’s the deal with all this pipe and stuff?”

“Whadda you mean?”

“Is it just for show? Like a cover for something else?”

“What the hell are you talkin’ about?

“Well, my guess is that Craven has planted a transmitter on the *Explorer* just like he did on the *Intrepid.* I’m wondering if Wray might be planning on dumping all of this so he can pick up a load of pot along the way and then sneak in behind the *Explorer.*”

“Do you care?”

“Not really. I’m just wondering if we might be rendezvousing with someone before we get to the Pacific. I’d like to know my escape options.”

“As far as I know, Wray won’t be stopping anywhere. Now quit bugging me, okay?”

He gave me a disgusting look and then walked away. I didn’t know what was bothering him, but I knew from then on, it wasn’t going to be me. Besides, he just told me all I needed to know.

By the time I relieved Craven at nine that night, I could see that Wray had charted our course through the southern Philippines and into the Pacific, passing north of Hawaii by about a hundred miles. It was almost the reciprocal course we had taken on the *Intrepid.* It was ideal. I could now calculate when we would be in prime position for me to act. I was going over those calculations with my back to the helm when I heard someone behind me. It was Wray.

“Whadda you doin’?”

"Just checking our course."

"Well, unless you messed with it, our course is fine." Wray looked over the control counsel, checking the compass heading and engine R.P.M.'s. When he bent over and put his head into the black hood of the radar, I realized how vulnerable he was in that position. It would be easy to club him over the head while he had his face buried in the radar.

Wray stood up and noticed me watching him. "The fuck you lookin' at?"

"Oh, nothin'." I suppressed a smile.

Wray smirked and then started down the ladder to the deck below. He stopped halfway and said, "Remember, I'll take care of our course, you watch the radar and try not to hit anything. I'll relieve you in an hour."

I watched his head disappear down the ladder before I looked at the nav chart again. We had already entered the Sulu Sea and were nearing the Philippines. My first chance to kill the bastard was now less than twenty-four hours away.

The next day after I got off watch, I dropped down to the galley. With no one around, I started putting a survival kit together. I filled two plastic jugs with water and rummaged around until I found a half dozen granola bars and put them in a plastic bag. I grabbed another Ziploc bag that I would put my money and passport in. Before going on the evening watch I would take these things to the Zodiac and slip them under the cover. I would check the fuel line and gas once more and then leave half of the cover unsnapped. I figured I would be able to do all of this out of sight of the cameras.

When I was satisfied I had my survival kit together, I headed off to the engine room. There was still one more thing that I would need before my watch that evening. The Crescent wrench that I had earlier should do the trick.

CHAPTER FORTY-SEVEN

The Philippine Islands

The next night, on the way to the bridge to stand, what I hoped to be, my last watch aboard the *Gladiator,* I quietly stashed my supplies in the Zodiac and unsnapped a few of the fasteners on the boats` cover. Once inside the bridge, I relieved Craven and then placed the Crescent wrench below the chart table. Everything was in position. All I could do then, was wait.

Three agonizing hours later, at 11:45pm, Wray entered the wheelhouse. It was finally time to kill the son of a bitch.

Wray didn't say anything as he walked over and looked down at the control console. The red glow from the instrument panel's lights reflected off his face, giving him an even more sinister look. When he did look up, he turned to me and said, "Okay, you're relieved. I've got the helm."

As soon as Wray turned his attention back to the control board, I eased around the chart table and picked up the wrench in my right hand. My hand started to shake as I stepped back around the table and positioned myself directly behind him. My breathing quickened and my brain started screaming.

Now!

HIT THIS FUCKER... NOW!!

Wray lifted his head and stared straight ahead at my reflection in the glass of the windscreen. "I said you're relieved Tatcher. Go below."

I stood there like a statue for a long moment, frozen in time. Then, before I knew what I was doing, I blurted out, "Tim Williams!"

Wray stood there, watching my reflection. "What? What the fuck you talkin' about? Who's Tim Williams?"

"Tim Williams. He was my brother." Flushed and shaking, I stepped to the man's left to confront him face to face.

"Well, good for you," Wray smirked. "Now get out of my way, I wanna look at the radar."

My heart pounded as Wray walked around me and bent over the radar. The voice in my head was screaming so loud that I almost didn't hear what Wray said next.

"Holy shit! What the hell's goin' on out there?" Wray said with his head still buried in the hood of the radar. Then he stood up and looked at me. "Have you seen what's on the screen?"

Before I could say anything, he stuck his head back toward the radar.

Hit him! Hit him NOW goddammit!

"There's all kind of shit in front of us," Wray said, still with his head under the hood. Whadda you think they are? Fishin' boats or something?"

A second passed before the screaming in my head gave way to an image in my mind of...*fishing boats.* I flashed back to the night on the *Intrepid* when we had first entered Philippine waters and encountered all the small boats and canoes. I pushed Wray away and looked at the green screen for myself.

"Yeah, they're fishing boats alright. Very small."

"How small?"

Almost in a trance I said, "Twenty feet maybe. Some even smaller. Canoes."

"Canoes? They wouldn't show up on radar would they?"

"No, they wouldn't. We're probably only seeing about half of what's really out there."

"Well, goddammit, we'll be dodging these fucks all night! Stupid bastards. Whadda they doin' anyway. They shouldn't be out here in those tiny fuckin' things."

"They're just trying to feed their families," I said, as my shaking began to subside. "They're just trying to stay alive."

Wray stared at me as my words hung in the air. My breathing slowed and my shoulders slumped. I realized the moment that I had waited for, for so long, had come and gone. If I killed Wray and abandoned the bridge, the *Gladiator* would just plow through all those fishermen out there in the dark.

I stood there a few seconds letting my heart rate settle down. And in those few moments something else became very clear to me; I was never going to be able to kill Wray. I didn't have it in me.

Finally I took a deep breath and made my way to the ladder leading to the galley below. I left Wray muttering to himself about his misfortune.

As I passed through the galley I saw Jimeen sitting at the table, a cup of coffee in front of him. He looked up at me. "You off watch now?"

I nodded slowly."Yeah, I'm off."

We stared at each other until Jimeen asked, "Did you use that?"

For a second I didn't know what he was talking about, then I looked down at the wrench that was still in my right hand. "No...I couldn't do it.

I thought I saw a slight smile just before Jimeen raised his coffee to his lips. When he looked away and didn't say anything else, I turned and headed below to my bunk.

In the passageway below, I could hear Craven snoring loudly. As I entered the cabin I made sure I slammed the door, and then for good measure I stepped hard on Craven's mattress before settling in roughly on the bunk above him. His snoring sputtered to a stop.

As I laid in my bunk in the dark, an overwhelming feeling of despair washed over me. The moment of truth had come and I had failed. Not only did I not have it in me to kill Wray, I probably jeopardized my situation by blurting out Tim's name. Wray acted as if he didn't know who I was talking about, and maybe he didn't, but I couldn't be sure that at some point he might put it together. I remembered what the German sailor had said about the pistol in Wray's room. I was going to have to watch my back.

My thoughts turned to my brother and I began to feel that I would have his blessing for not extracting revenge. I was sure that he would rather see me save myself and let karma catch up to Wray. I realized that I needed to go ahead with my escape plan, and the sooner the better.

I decided I would wait for Jimeen to relieve Wray on his watch, then after Wray went to his cabin, I'd wait an hour and then make my break. I could only hope that Jimeen wouldn't interfere. Even if Wray was still awake and heard something, I'd be gone by the time he reached the boat deck. It had to work. We wouldn't be near land for another seven thousand miles.

CHAPTER FORTY-EIGHT

The next night I stood my watch under a clear sky and the light of a half moon. The seas were fairly calm and I could see the silhouette of the Philippine Islands. Conditions were ideal. Wray relieved me early again saying, "I'm gonna take us through this passage, there's still too much shit too run into around here. In about three hours we'll be clear of the islands and into the Pacific. Nothing but open ocean the rest of the way."

As I looked at Wray, I hoped that at some point, the son of a bitch would know how close he came to dying and why.

When I left the bridge, I went outside and around to the boat deck. I wanted to check the air in the inflatable one more time. In about four hours I wanted to to be in it and heading towards the rest of my life.

When I approached the dingy, I froze...the cover had been refastened! Quickly I unsnapped a corner of the cover near the motor and pulled it back. My survival kit was gone! I pulled the cover back a little more and my heart stopped; the fuel line and oars were missing. Jimeen! I was frantic. Hurriedly I re-snapped the cover and went looking for Jimeen. I found him in the galley. I got right into his face before I said in a low growl, "*Now* what are you doing to me?!"

Jimeen looked around nervously and then said in a hushed voice, "Believe it or not Sonny, I'm trying to help you. I'm working on a plan that'll help you *and* me out of this mess."

"Yeah, great. How about letting me in on it then. What the hell are you doing?"

"Keep your voice down. I can't explain it all to you right now. You'll have to trust me. Just be patient and don't try to go anywhere."

"*Go* anywhere? That's funny. I don't have much of a choice now do I? I assume you have my passport too?"

Suddenly Wray yelled down from the bridge, "Hey! Down in the galley!" "How about a cup of coffee up here?"

Jimeen leaned into me and whispered, "Trust me," then headed for the coffee pot.

Like a whipped dog, I headed below to my bunk wondering if there would ever be justice for Wray or if I would ever know the truth about Kelli.

Sometime during the night I felt a change in the *Gladiator's* motion. Instead of a side-to-side roll, the ship was now pitching ever so slightly, and I knew why. We had cleared the Philippine Islands. The *Gladiator* was now responding to the swells of the Pacific Ocean.

The next day when I got up, land was nowhere in sight. A wave of depression hit me and I realized that I had no choice now but to hope that Jimeen was telling me the truth about some sort of a plan. I also had to to face the possibility of riding the boat all the way back to the States. If it came to that, and for some reason the U.S Coast Guard stopped us, at least I would have the satisfaction of telling the D.E.A. everything I knew about Wray. Whether that would be enough to convict him of anything I couldn't be sure. In fact, as far as his role on the *Gladiator* went, I couldn't see that Wray had done anything illegal.

Resigned to the fact that I was out of options for the time being, I continued my act as engineer. I made my usual rounds through the engine room and did some needed maintenance. I relieved Craven from his watches and put up with his usual sniveling about something. I quit looking at our course on the nav chart. There was nothing but thousands of miles of open ocean.

Hawaii would be the closest point of land on our plotted course, but we would miss the islands by a couple of hundred miles or so, to the south. The autopilot was set on seventy-eight degrees and probably wouldn't change for weeks. I had no choice but to wait, watch, and be careful.

About a week after clearing the Philippines, our radar mysteriously quit working. Wray called me to the wheelhouse to repair it, but he flew into a rage when I told him I didn't know much about electronics and couldn't fix it. I left him fuming on the bridge and went about my job as a sailor on a small ship crossing the Pacific, nothing more, nothing less. I was trying to stay numb while biding my time, waiting on Jimeen.

I avoided Wray and Craven as much as I could. I watched Jimeen for any kind of a signal, but it seemed like he was doing his best to avoid me. Then one day as I was coming out of the galley, I accidentally collided with him. He hesitated for a second and then exploded,"Goddammit, watch where you're going!!"

"Whoa, take it easy," I said.

"No, *you* take it easy. You get your head outta your ass, you won't be running into people!"

As I watched him walk away, I noticed Craven in the shadows of the galley, watching what just happened and grinning like an idiot.

In the days following the incident with Jimeen, he seemed to be gong out of his way to give me grief. During supper one night, I had just sat down to eat something that Craven had slapped together. It looked like rice and noodles and some vegetables I didn't recognize. Wray was carrying his plate up the ladder to the wheelhouse when he heard me ask Craven, "What is this?"

Before Craven could answer, Jimeen stopped and bellowed, "What's the matter Chief, don't you like the chow around here?"

"I was just asking what..."

"Yeah sure," Jimeen interrupted, "You fuckin' engineers are all alike. You got oil in your hair and grease under your fingernails, then you sit down to eat and you think things taste funny! Hah!"

"Hey," I started, "All I was…"

"Yeah right. Maybe we should let you do the cookin'?" Then he looked at Craven and smirked. "No we better not. He'd probably season everything with diesel fuel, give us all the shits!"

I let him go up the ladder without responding. I was losing patience with Jimeen.

As the days turned into weeks, Jimeen became more and more surly towards me, but only when Wray or Craven was around. On one especially contentious encounter, Jimeen even threatened to throw me overboard. After two weeks at sea, I decided I'd had enough.

Around 4 a.m. the next morning, when I was sure Wray had gone to bed, I quietly made my way up to the wheelhouse where Jimeen was standing watch. I wasn't going to take a chance on being overheard by Wray so I had a hand written note ready. It read simply: "Bullshit!! What's going on? Please?"

I took a pen with me and as softly as I could, I started up to the wheelhouse. Halfway up the ladder I heard the faint crackle of the VHF radio.

Several seconds went by as I waited on the ladder, then I heard Jimeen in a hushed voice say, "See see." A second later I heard what sounded like a mike being keyed twice, *Click, click.* Then Jimeen again: "One six five degrees, nine minutes west. Two eight degrees, two minutes north. Copy?"

This time I thought I heard a faint voice answer: "See see," followed by some other coordinates I couldn't quite hear.

I let a minute pass in silence before I climbed the rest of the way into the wheelhouse.

Jimeen jumped when he saw me but I quickly stuffed the pen and note in his hand so he'd know that I wasn't there for a verbal confrontation.

Looking relieved, Jimeen read the note, nodded, then turned it over and scribbled on the back of it. He handed it back to me and watched my face for a reaction. The note read: "Very soon now. Will know in 24hrs."

When I looked up from the note, Jimeen raised his eyebrows and gave me a thumbs up.

I shook my head in resignation and went below.

I was on watch at 11:45 a.m. when Wray climbed into the wheelhouse and went straight to the navigation table. After about ten minutes of figuring and calculating he said his first words to me since arriving on the bridge that morning. "Okay, I've got it."

The first thing he did when he took over the helm was to nudge the throttles up just a bit. When he saw me watching him he said, "I'm increasing the R.P.M.'s by a couple hundred. Don't anybody screw with `em."

He didn't have to tell me twice. I quickly left him alone on the bridge and went to the engine room to do some more maintenance.

I knew the primary fuel tanks had probably accumulated some water and I needed to drain them off. After I changed out a couple of fuel filters I put them in a bag to toss overboard. When I came back out of the engine room, I saw Jimeen step out of the galley and look around. He saw me and headed my way. I started to throw the trash overboard when Jimeen yelled, "Hey! Wait a minute."

I sat the trash bag down on the railing and waited. When he drew near enough he asked, "Look behind me. Anybody watching us?"

I looked over his shoulder at the bridge and boat deck. I knew Wray didn't usually have the cameras on during the day, but I said, "No, not unless Wray powered up the cameras."

"Good, listen, I've been in radio contact…"

"Yeah, I heard," I interrupted.

"You did?"

"Yeah, I was coming up to the wheelhouse the other night and I overheard you."

"Alright, I'll explain more about that in a minute. Right now I need to know what you did with that box of spare parts I brought aboard when I first got here."

"I put it under the control board in the engine room."

"Good, okay, here's what I want you to do. If you dig through the parts on top of the box, you'll find a bundle near the bottom. Don't take the cover off it or anything, just take it out and put it in a trash bag, but don't secure the top. And make sure you do it out of range of the camera down there."

"Yeah, sure, no problem."

"Then leave it in the engine room where you can get to it in a hurry if you have to."

"Okay, but what's in…?"

"Hey, Al." It was Craven yelling down from the boat deck. I hadn't seen him come out of the wheelhouse.

"Al," Craven yelled again. "The captain would like a word with you."

Jimeen turned and waved up at Craven."I'll be right there." When he turned back to me he asked, "Is he still there? Is he still watching us?"

I glanced over Jimeen`s shoulder and saw that Craven hadn't moved from his perch.

"Yeah, still there."

"Good, be in the wheelhouse at 3:30 tomorrow morning. I'll fill you in on everything."

Then, without warning, Jimeen jabbed a finger in my chest and in a loud voice said, "And like I told you before, you gotta poke holes in these bags so they'll sink before you toss `em. Get that in your head or I'll toss you!"

Jimeen turned and headed back towards the galley. My eyes drifted up to Craven. He was grinning again like the idiot I knew he was. I gave him the finger and started off to the engine room.

I went straight to the box in the engine room and lifted out some strange-looking parts I'd never seen before and set them aside. Near the bottom of the box I saw the bundle that Jimeen had described. I couldn't tell what it was for sure but I noticed a small lanyard coiled on top of the bundle with a clip at the end of it. There were some letters stamped on the cover: 'F.A.A. Certified'.

What the hell is this? A parachute?

I was curious as hell, but I figured I'd better not mess with it. Mindful of the engine room camera, I took it out and placed it in a trash bag then set it just under the ladder leading out of the engine room. If Jimeen was telling the truth, I'd find out soon enough what it was. Until then I could only stay in the mode I'd been in for so long…watch, wait, and be patient.

CHAPTER FORTY-NINE

163 degrees, 6 minutes West.
24 degrees, 3 minutes North.
3:30 am

Sleep had been out of the question since getting off watch at midnight. I lay in my bunk and looked at my watch every five minutes. Finally, at 3:30, I quietly let myself out of the cabin and headed topside. It was a clear, moonless night and the stars seemed to be especially bright.

Just as I was passing through the galley, Jimeen practically knocked me over coming down the ladder from the wheelhouse. "Goddammit," he said in a loud whisper. "Somebody kicked up our speed!"

"Yeah, Wray did."

"Shit. When did he... never mind. You got that bag ready?"

"Yeah."

"Good, go grab it and meet me amidships, starboard side, soon as you can. Hurry!"

The urgency in Jimeen`s voice sent me flying to the engine room. I grabbed the bag and hustled back up to the aft deck, arriving at the designated spot just as Jimeen did.

Breathlessly Jimeen squinted his eyes from the deck light and said, "Okay, we're gettin' outta here. Set that bag down on the rail between us but keep your back to the wheelhouse. Don't turn around."

He was starting to make me nervous.

"Okay, there's a small raft in this bag, the kind some airlines used, and what I'm about to do is for the sake of the camera."

Suddenly he flew into a pantomime rage, pointing and gesturing to the trash bag. He stuck his right hand into the bag while he jabbed me in the chest with his left. Then in a move so fast I almost didn't see it, he dropped his left hand to my belt buckle and yanked me toward him. A split second later his right hand came out of the bag with one end of the lanyard and in a flash, he clipped it through one of my belt loops. Still in an animated fury he stuck his face in mine and said under his breath. "Okay, you're tied to the raft, now when you hit the water, count to ten and pull the cord. You got it?"

"Raft? Hit the water? What the hell are you talking…?"

"Goddammit, I don't have time to explain!" Jimeen grabbed me by both hands and began wrestling me towards the railing.

My first instinct was to resist and I did. "Get the hell off me. What're you---"

Then, with a strength I had felt from him once before, he lifted my feet off the deck and bent me backwards over the rail. The bundle fell over as I grabbed Jimeen in a headlock. I held onto him with all my strength but couldn't stop our momentum and we both went overboard. As we went over the side I felt my head hit the side of the boat a split second before smashing face down into the sea. I felt the wake of the *Gladiator* push me away from the boat as I rolled over on my back. I lay stunned in the water for several seconds before I felt my eyes stinging and the taste of salt water. I began coughing and choking. Half-conscious, I fought to stay afloat but I could feel myself getting weaker.

Ten…something about counting to ten. Maybe if I just count to ten…

I could see the lights of the *Gladiator* growing dimmer. *One… two…three…*My lights dimmed completely before I reached four.

CHAPTER FIFTY

"Sonny? Sonny can you hear me?"

I slowly opened my eyes and saw the faces of two identical women staring at me.

I closed my eyes and rested again. I could hear a soft creaking and felt an easy floating motion beneath me.

When I opened my eyes for the second time, I saw the same two women, but then I blinked and they became one.

"Hello, Sonny," the face said.

The woman looked vaguely familiar. I blinked again. She appeared to be Asian, maybe in her mid-forties. She had beautiful light brown skin and her face was framed by flowing black hair. Her eyes were dark brown and had a soft look about them. When she smiled her lips spread back over dazzling white teeth. She was very pretty.

"Can you hear me?" she asked.

I looked into her coal black eyes. "Am I dead?"

"No," she said and laughed, "you're very much alive."

I looked around at my immediate surroundings. I was lying on a bunk and could see blue sky through a hatch above me. Everything seemed to be tilted at a funny angle.

"Where am I? How'd I get here?"

"You're aboard the sloop, *Si, Sea Rider*. We plucked you and Al out of the water hours ago."

A face appeared in the hatch above me, it was upside down but I could tell that it was Jimeen.

"How's the patient? Or should I say prisoner?" He laughed.

"He's awake and doing good honey, come on down and see for yourself."

Jimeen`s face disappeared for a second then reappeared right side up as he moved down the steps from the hatch.

The woman helped me sit up on the edge of the bunk as Jimeen asked, "How ya doin`, sailor?"

I winched a little as I felt the knot on the side of my head. "Okay, I guess. A little groggy maybe."

"I bet you are. You took quite a shot when we went overboard. Sorry `bout that."

Bits of recollections started filtering through and I remembered being on the deck of the *Gladiator* with Jimeen.

"The *Gladiator*? Where…is she? What happened?" I tried to shake the cobwebs away.

"Not to worry son, Wray and the *Gladiator* are miles away from us, and as far as I know, still steaming toward San Francisco."

"San Francisco?" I could feel a throbbing in my head coming on strong. I suddenly felt nauseous. "What's goin` on?"

"Don't worry…you're not…"

The woman interrupted, "Look, honey, I think Sonny better lie back down for awhile. You guys`ll have all the time in the world to talk about things later. Best he gets some more rest for now."

I didn't argue with the lovely lady as she helped me lie back down. "When you feel like getting up," she added, "I've put some dry shorts and a tee shirt here by the bunk. If you need to use the head, it's forward, port side." I closed my eyes and felt the throbbing in my head begin to subside. There was no sound other than the soft creaking of the boat. Just before I slipped back into dreamland, the woman placed a cool cloth on my forehead.

Why did she seem so familiar?

When I awoke later, I was alone. The deck was still tilted at the same angle but I could see the shadows had moved. I vaguely remembered an angel had said something about being aboard a sloop or something like that. A gimbal cup holder above a cooktop swayed with a gentle motion and I could hear the sounds of wind and water flowing by outside. Gingerly, I sat up on the edge of the bunk and felt my head. The pain had abated to a mild headache. I could hear voices outside the hatch speaking softly.

After a moment or two, I felt strong enough to slip into the shorts the woman had laid out for me. As I slid them on I could see that they were maybe a size too big but they would do fine. Finally I stood up and tried my sea legs. They were a little shaky but with some effort I was able to make it over to the small ladder that led up through the hatch and topside.

At the base of the ladder, I took a deep breath, steadied myself, then climbed the first two steps and peeked outside. From my position on the steps I couldn't see much forward other than a large spiked wheel, a cowling and an instrument panel. But looking aft, I could see that a Bimini convertible cloth top had been folded, and Jimeen and the woman I'd seen before were relaxing in the sunshine. Jimeen was shirtless, shoeless, and wearing the same kind of shorts I had on. The woman was barefoot and wore shorts and a tank top; I couldn't help but notice her tanned, slender legs. Her right hand rested causally on Jimeen`s thigh. Since neither one of them seemed to be steering the boat, I assumed we were on autopilot.

"Well look who's with us," the woman said as she noticed me standing on the ladder. "How are you feeling now?"

"Okay, I guess," I said as I felt my head. "Better…I think."

Jimeen gave me a wave and said, "Good, come on up here and I'll introduce you."

I took the remaining steps up and out to the deck as Jimeen said, "Sonny, this is the special lady that I've been in love with for a long, long time. Sonny, say hello to Loraine."

The woman stood up and extended her hand; "So nice to finally meet you Sonny, I've heard a lot of good things about you."

I immediately liked the woman. She seemed to have a grace and warmth about her that went well with her friendly smile.

As I stood there looking at the two of them, their smiles seemed to grow larger and soon they were grinning like Cheshire cats. Finally, Jimeen said with a nod of his head, "And Sonny, I think you already know our daughter, the one standing behind you."

Confused, I slowly turned around and looked toward the bow. My heart immediately jammed in my throat. Standing on the other side of the helm not four feet from me was…Kelli!

She was even more beautiful than I remembered.

I tried to swallow… I tried to speak…I could do neither.

Just then a wave lifted the boat, my already unstable legs turned to Jello, and I fell hard on the cockpit bench.

"Oh Sonny," Kelli cried as she jumped down into the cockpit. I sat up quickly as Jimeen and Loraine moved to steady me. Kelli knelt in front of me with a worried look in her eyes. Still speechless, I stared into her eyes. Slowly, tenderly, she took my face in her hands. I watched as tears started down her cheeks and she slowly moved her head from side to side.

"Oh Sonny…Sonny," she moaned, "I was so afraid I'd never see you again."

My heart was pounding away, and still I couldn't say a word.

Kelli stared into my eyes and said, "I'm so sorry about your brother. I'm so sorry for everything you've been through."

She began looking at the cuts and bruises on my face, touching them gently.

Then she looked in my eyes and asked, "Are you ever going to say anything?"

I closed my eyes and shook my head, trying to snap my brain in gear. *I hit my head. I must have a concussion.* When I opened my eyes again, she was still there, right in front of me. Loraine and Jimeen were on either side of her. I swallowed a couple of times and finally found my voice. "Wha…what're you doing here? I…I can't believe it. Where did you come from? How can this be happening?"

"Oh, Sonny, the only thing that's important right now is that you and my father are safe. That's what we've been praying for."

Slowly I took one of her hands in mine and kissed her palm. *She was real, this was actually happening!* I heard Loraine say something to Jimeen and they quietly went below.

A jillion questions were swimming in my head but they would have to wait for now. I was just happy to be alive with a real angel kneeling in front of me.

"You came back Sonny," she said tenderly. "I prayed you would."

Without taking my eyes off of her I blurted out, "I came back to kill a man."

"I know." She took my hand over and held it to her lips.

"A man I once thought you might be…"

"Wray? No, I never knew him. I only found out recently that he's been blackmailing my father."

I didn't say anything, but I could feel a smile was taking over my face.

"I like your new look," she said as she touched my chin again. "But your face is a mess."

"Well," I grimaced," I doubt if we can find a doctor who'll make a house call out here."

"No," she smiled coyly, "but I know a nurse who will."

She stood up and pulled me to her. We slid into each other's arms, hearts pounding. She kissed me softly on my neck and breathed, "I love you Sonny."

"I love you too," I said as I kissed her ear. "I never stopped."

We held each other and swayed together as the *Si, Sea Rider* sliced through the sea.

CHAPTER FIFTY-ONE

"Hello up there," Loraine said as she popped her head up through the hatch. "You guys hungry? I've got some grub ready if you'd like."

Kelli put her hands on my chest and turned her head to her mother. "Sure Mom, you want some help?"

"No that's okay, there's an old sailor down here that won't keep his hands to himself. I'll send him up in a minute."

I suddenly realized I was starving.

Kelli turned back to me and I asked, "How long was I out? How long have I been aboard?"

"Well, lets see…we plucked you guys out of the water about four this morning…and it's about eleven now, so what's that… seven hours I guess."

I shook my head, trying to digest the turn of events and marveling at the magnificent boat I was now on. I took a step up from the cockpit and could see a weathered teak deck splitting the cabin structure and running the length of the boat which I guessed to be about fifty feet. A tall single mast proudly rose up to anchor a huge mainsail and foresail which at the time, were filled with the winds of the Pacific powering us through the sea.

"Whose boat is this anyway?" I asked.

"It's my fathers`. He bought it a couple of years ago and kept it moored in Hawaii. Mom moved aboard not long ago and has been taking care of it. We left Honolulu about ten days ago."

"You sailed this boat from Hawaii…to meet the *Gladiator*?"

"Well yes, something like that."

"How? How did you do it?"

"I told you my dad taught me to sail when I was a kid. He taught my mom…"

"No, no, I mean, how'd you know where we`d be? How did you find us?"

"We've been plotting your course. We've been in radio contact with…"

"Okay, gather `round for the catch of the day," Jimeen said as he stepped out from the hatch balancing a serving tray. Loraine followed with a pitcher of lemonade and four plastic cups. Loraine motioned for us to sit, and then they both set their offerings on the deck in front of us.

"Hope you like mahi mahi, Sonny," Loraine said as she set a paper plate on my knee. "Kelli caught it this morning, while you guys were, ah...resting."

"I love fish." I looked at my plate, then at all of them. I felt like a king. "It's all wonderful…I …I really don't know what to say."

"Well shut up and eat then." Jimeen laughed and everybody started in on the fish.

Ten minutes later, Loraine noticed my empty plate and asked, "More fish Sonny?"

I started to protest mildly but she wouldn't have it.

"Here, have what's left of mine," she said as she slid what was left of her portion onto my plate. "I can't eat all of it, besides, I know where we can get more. Especially now that there's some real fishermen aboard." She settled back against the cushions, pulling her knees up, and smiling as she rested her head on Jimeen`s shoulder.

I could see where Kelli got her beauty. Loraine's skin tone, white teeth and dimpled smile were all replicated in her daughter.

When I looked at Jimeen I could tell I was looking at a truly happy man. I almost didn't want to take a chance of disturbing his state of bliss or mine by saying anything or asking any questions, but I had to...I had to ask. I shook my head slowly, still in wonderment and asked, "Al…how and why did all this happen? You *did* throw me off the *Gladiator* didn't you?"

He smiled. "Well, yes I did. I had planned on telling you what was going on before we went over the side, but things happened so fast I didn't have time."

"Look you guys have a lot to talk about," Loraine interrupted. So…" She stood up and began collecting the lunch ware. Kelli immediately took her cue and moved to help her. When they had everything gathered up, they headed for the hatch. On the way, Loraine stopped and kissed Jimeen on top of his head. He responded with a gentle squeeze on the back of her bare leg. Kelli looked back at me and smiled, and then both women went below.

Jimeen and I watched the women disappear, both of us smiling in contentment.

"Well, Sonny, I think everything is going to work out," Jimeen began. "I've been looking forward to this day for so long, I can't tell you how good I feel right now."

"I think I have a pretty good idea Al, I can see it on your face."

"Yeah, well it's been a long time coming."

I let him savor the moment a little longer then I reminded him, "Al…you were about to tell me how this all happened, how we got here."

I watched his smile fade slowly then he began slowly, "Yeah, well Sonny, it's kind of a long story, but you're certainly entitled to some answers, so here goes. You remember what I told you about Wray blackmailing me in the beginning and all, and why I couldn't go to the police? Well, after my wife died, I really did think about going to the feds. I thought about turning myself in. But then I thought about Loraine and Kelli. They both knew about my wife all along, I was honest with them about that, but neither knew anything about what I was involved in. I didn't want to hurt them and I also couldn't bear the thought of not seeing either one of them for god-knows-how-long if I turned myself in."

Jimeen shook his head, sucked in a deep breath, and looked out to sea. I was almost sorry I had asked him to explain anything.

"Finally I talked with Loraine and told her everything. She was shocked at first of course, but then she said she'd stand beside me, whatever decision I made. I hated the thought of Kelli knowing her father was a drug smuggler, but still, I considered going to the feds. Well, Wray must have sensed this because one day I got a phone call from one of his scumbags, I think it was Craven. He said something like, `So sorry to hear about your wife, but you still have that beautiful daughter. You must be very proud of her, being a nurse and all. It would be a pity if any of her own blood ever stained that nice white uniform.` Well, that did it right there. I knew I could never go to the police."

I could imagine Craven saying those things and felt bile rising in my throat. I stood up and spit over the side. Jimeen waited until I sat back down.

"For years I'd been skimming from the top of Wray's drug deals. His profits were enormous and he never noticed. I took enough to make me a wealthy man, although it didn't help my heart any. I was hoping that one day there would be an opportunity to use that money to make an escape. After the threatening phone call, I went back to planning that escape. I figured if Wray *thought* I was dead, then that would be the end of it, so I planned on killing myself."

Jimeen laughed at my reaction.

"Not actually doing it of course, but faking it in a way that Wray would believe I was really dead. I thought maybe if I could be aboard one of his drug runs, I could `accidentally` fall overboard and get lost at sea. It would really have to be convincing and of course I would need someone to pick me up before I was really lost at sea. So I bought this boat in Hawaii and upgraded her with all the latest electronic equipment with that thought in mind.

"When I told Loraine what I was planning, she was a little skeptical at first but thought it could work. You see, when I first met Loraine, I took her sailing one day and she loved it. After that, we'd go sailing whenever we had time. After awhile, she was able to handle a boat as well as anybody."

At that moment, as if to prove his point, Loraine stuck her head up from below and eyed the sea and the sails. "Looks like the wind's picking up a bit," she said. "It's been doing that about this time every day since we've been at sea. You think we should let out more sail? Maybe tweak her starboard a few clicks…Captain?"

"Captain?" Jimeen laughed. "I thought you were the captain!"

"No, I'm the first and forever mate," she answered. "And don't you forget it!"

"Whatever you say, sweetheart. You want some help?"

"No, it looks like you boys are in a deep discussion, I'll get it." She nimbly jumped up on the deck and went about her business. I could feel the boat respond to her tweaking as we heeled over slightly and picked up speed. A few moments later, satisfied we were in the right configuration, Loraine arranged some cushions from a forward locker, gave us a wave and stretched out on the foredeck, book in hand.

"Goddamn, I love that woman," Jimeen said, his eyes glistening. A minute passed before he said anything else. Finally he cleared his throat and continued.

"Anyway, like I was saying, I was trying to figure out how to make my plan work. The difficult part would be in communicating with Loraine and coordinating a pick-up spot. I wasn`t about to jump off a boat at night in the middle of the ocean unless I knew Loraine was within a half mile, and I didn't want anyone else to know there was another ship in the area in case there was an investigation later. I would need to disable our radar in a way that nobody could use it except me when I needed it. I didn't want anybody looking at the radar and seeing another boat so close to us. These things were all do-able but still the main challenge would be to get Loraine to within that half mile. Then when I found out that Wray and Craven were setting up decoy loads with tracking devices, it gave me an idea. If I could get a transmitter, or tracking device like Craven was using, and bring it aboard with me, Loraine could track me right up until I could see her on the radar screen. But I knew those transmitters only had a battery life of about thirty days, so, as a back-up plan, and to make sure Loraine was close, I'd want to make radio contact with her. She needed my exact longitude and latitude. Like I said, there are no street signs out here."

"No shit," I said, looking around at an empty ocean.

"Well, I was still working out some things in my head when Wray had me broker the deal to bring back some oil drilling equipment. I didn't think much about it until he told me he was going to bring the ship back himself. And then you entered the picture with the tragic death of your brother. I could see you wanted Wray dead and I certainly couldn't blame you. I'm embarrassed now to think how easy I made it possible for you to seek revenge. I hope some day you might forgive me for that... and for my role that lead to your brother's death."

Jimeen looked at me for a reaction, but needing to forgive him for anything seemed laughable at that point.

"Right after you got out of the country, I called Loraine. I told her our problem was probably solved, that there was someone who would take care of Wray for us. I told her all about you and asked her what she thought about the new developments. That's when she laid a bombshell on me. I didn't know it, but Kelli had confided in her mother about a young American sailor that she had met and fallen in love with months earlier. She was sure he was going to come back for her. That man, of course was you. That's when I knew our problem wasn't solved at all. Not yet anyway.

"So I decided to go ahead with my phony death plan, but I thought about bringing you into it as well. I immediately called the radio operator that was supposed to go with you guys and told him the trip had been canceled. I knew Wray didn't know squat about electronic gear or hardly anything about radio frequencies, so I knew he'd have to take me aboard when I showed up.

"I called Loraine and told her to send for Kelli immediately, get her out of Labuan however she could, and get ready to sail. I was thinking I would include you in my escape plan for my daughter's sake. Now, you're probably wondering why

I didn't tell you right away what I was up to, but I gotta tell you Sonny, I love my daughter with all my heart, and frankly, I wasn't sure I wanted her mixed up with, well…a killer. And Sonny, like it or not, that's what you would've been had you tossed Wray.

"So, I decided to wait and see what you were going to do. If you killed Wray, fine, I was off the hook, you would disappear, and I could only hope my daughter would get over you.

"But you didn't kill Wray, you couldn't. That's when I knew my daughter was probably in love with the right man. I was gonna let you in on my plan when I thought the time was right but, I thought it best to give Wray and Craven the impression that you and me didn't get along very well. I thought it would come in handy later if Wray and Craven ever had to testify about our disappearance.

"Well, I knew we were getting real close to Loraine and Kelli last night but didn't realize Wray had increased our speed. When I turned on the radar I damned near had a heart attack! The `*Rider* was just off our starboard bow! We had to get off in a hurry. Sorry I didn't have time to tell you what was goin` on," Jimeen said as he grimaced slightly and rubbed the back of his neck, "but I think our little scene was pretty well acted out!"

"No kidding" I said, feeling the side of my head. "You must have got me in the raft then, the one you clipped me to?"

"Yeah, at least you didn't put up a fight then, thank God."

I thought about that a little then asked, "So when Wray searches the ship and sees we're missing, he'll probably check the cameras, is that it?"

"You got it."

"And he'll see that we went overboard…lost at sea?"

"Yep."

It took me awhile to digest what he'd told me, and then I thought of Wray and the *Gladiator*. I looked down at the deck and said, "I still can't believe what's happening here. I'm really grateful to you Al, for what you've done, but tell me, what happens to Wray now? What's he up to? Does he just sail away?"

"No he doesn't just sail away. In fact," Jimeen said with a gleam in his eye, "Butch Wray's adventure is just beginning."

"Yeah? How so?"

"Just before I left the States, I found out what Wray was really up to. He wasn't just bringing oil drilling equipment back as cargo, he *was* bringing a load of drugs."

"Drugs? I thought you said he wasn't picking up anything once he left Labuan?"

"He's not. He took on his load while you guys were in the shipyard in Labuan."

"I don't get it. What are you saying?"

"Sonny, there's enough heroin in those drill pipes to buy a good-sized country. A load of pot pales in comparison, dollar-wise."

It took a moment for it to sink in. "Well, I'll be damned. That sonofabitch!" I said.

When I looked at Jimeen again his smile was getting bigger.

"Well, hold on Sonny, because I think you're gonna like this part…you see, just before I came aboard the *Gladiator,* I made a stop at the *Explorer.* I knew the captain from when I set up the money for his load, so it didn't seem out of place for me to make a last minute call on him. Plus I brought a bag aboard with some current magazines and that sort of stuff. He told me about the quarantine so I figured Craven had already been aboard and planted the transmitter. I didn't say anything to the captain, but while I was on board, I used the head and sure enough, I found the transmitter in just about the same place he'd put it on your boat. Well, I stuffed it into the bag I'd brought with me, wished the captain luck, and left."

"Wait a minute," I said, "You're saying you took the transmitter from the *Explorer* and then brought it aboard the *Gladiator*?"

"Yep."

"And it's still aboard the *Gladiator?*"

"That's right. I assume the U.S. government is tracking it as we speak."

I was speechless. It was beautiful.

Neither of us said anything for a moment then Jimeen cleared his throat and said, "And I wouldn't be surprised if the same coast guard crew that boarded you guys on the *Intrepid* is already in position and waiting for Wray and the *Gladiator.* The coasties love this kind of a bust, you know, heroin and all. "

It finally became clear to me; not only would Jimeen and I no longer exist in the eyes of the authorities, but Wray and Craven were heading straight into the arms of the U.S. Coast Guard and DEA.

"Oh yeah, another thing," Jimeen said as he stood up and put a hand on my shoulder. "I anonymously sent the cops the video-tape of Wray with your brother in my garage. I included a note that suggested they re-open their investigation into the death of Tim Williams."

I couldn't hold my emotions in any longer. I stood up and grabbed Jimeen in a bear hug. The man had had a plan alright! We were still in an embrace when Kelli lifted her head out of the hatch. "Dad? I've been watching the *Gladiator* on the radar. She's still heading for San Francisco and almost out of range. Should we change course now?"

"Sure, sweetheart, let's head for Mexico."

"Mexico?" I asked.

"Yeah, I figure we'll shoot for Baja, then work our way down the coast. You see, Sonny, years ago I took some of Wray's money and invested in small marina with forty acres along the beach in Costa Rica. It's really beautiful there and the people are warm and friendly. I figured that any country that didn't have a need for a military is all right with me. I always hoped that someday I could retire there. Well, everyone I love is aboard this boat, and..."

Jimeen paused as Kelli worked her way up to the deck and stood beside me.

"...and we'll need help runnin' the place down there Sonny," Jimeen went on. "So whadda you say? Costa Rica all right with you?"

Kelli looked up at me then melted her body against mine. I kissed her neck and felt her warm tears on my shoulder. Neither one of us could speak.

Jimeen finally coughed and said, "I'll take that as a 'si, señor.' Welcome to the family, Sonny."

EPILOGUE

The hammock moved gently in the warm breeze. A few chickens strutted around, quietly pecking at the ground. A wild parrot squawked as the surf murmured beyond the lagoon. I felt Kelli stir beside me.

"Sonny?" she asked softly.

"Yeah?"

"Do you miss home?"

"Home? My home is here. With you and your family."

Kelli traced her fingers along my stomach."Someday we could have a family of our own you know. Would you like that Sonny?"

I smiled and kissed the top of her head. "Sure."

"And if we had a boy, we could name him after your brother."

"I'd like that."

A rooster fluffed himself up against one of the hens and suddenly there was a little dust-up. Loud squawking was followed by some serious clucking, but soon peace prevailed again.

We swayed in silence for awhile and then Kelli lifted her head and kissed my neck. "Hearing about Wray being indicted on all those charges was good news, wasn't it?"

"Yeah it was," I said. "Wray will get everything he's got comin`to him, especially if he runs into any of those guys he helped send to prison, the ones he set up. I'm sure Cal would like to see him."

"Wray`s finally getting what he deserves," Kelli said, as she eased her leg over mine and kissed me. "And so are you."

Made in the USA
Charleston, SC
19 February 2013